THE LAYERS

Stephen Reynolds was born in West Sussex in 1978. Since then, he has lived in Brighton, Portsmouth and London, and now lives in Bristol with his partner, Natasha. Stephen is an avid hiker and in 2017 he published a non-fiction title about his on-foot adventures, *Just Off For A Walk*, and has written several others since then.

The Layers

STEPHEN REYNOLDS

Valley Press

First published in 2021 by Valley Press
Woodend, The Crescent, Scarborough, YO11 2PW
www.valleypressuk.com

ISBN 978-1-912436-59-0
Cat. no. VP0180

A CIP record for this book is available from the British Library.

Cover and text design by Peter Barnfather.
Cover illustration (*Head of a Man, Full Face*) by Alphonse Legros
[courtesy National Gallery of Art, Washington].
Edited by Sam Keenaghan.

Printed and bound in Great Britain by
Imprint Digital, Upton Pyne, Exeter.

For my family. Past, present and future – I love you all. You are the light. You are not in this book and neither am I. Some of you may recognise a few of our protagonist's characteristics, both physical and emotional. Fragments of you all that I have stolen, without your consent, so as to put flesh on the bones of the souls that exist only within this story. Siblings, parents, grandparents, step-parents, partners and all the rest of you, shovelled into a blender, blitzed until almost unrecognisable and then poured back out onto the page. Likewise, you might just find that one or two anecdotes or stories awaken in you some long-forgotten memory. Familiar but not *quite* right. Plundered, disassembled, remoulded and then used to fill the potholes of this long and bumpy road. You are not in this book, but without you, what would it be, really?

PART ONE

Large electric bulbs bathe the street in an unnatural carica-
ture of sunlight. Familiar neon symbols glare out from
above the rows of gleaming glass shopfronts. Metal benches
coated in vandal-proof red paint sit bolted to the ground at
precisely measured-out intervals. An elderly woman sits
staring at a blank space as if it holds secrets that only she
can see. Bodies fill the space in a flowing, pulsing mass of
resignation. A mother grabs the arm of a small child and
swings him round to face her. A sinewy manicured finger
points down at the grubby little face as the tears begin to
flow. There is a constant murmur and hum of voices but
nobody is speaking. Each journey is self-contained, isolated
and straight-faced. A security guard stands in a doorway
with arms folded and legs apart. He's staring but his eyes
are glazed and unseeing; he is somewhere else, far away
from this place. Images of smooth smiling faces on video
display advertising boards fade in and out, in and out. Of
the hour or the season, there is no suggestion. Full of
people, emptied of life; a circus with no acts. I wipe the
corner of my mouth with the back of my hand and force
myself to focus on walking towards the automatic doors.

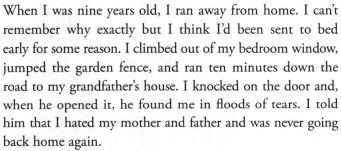

When I was nine years old, I ran away from home. I can't remember why exactly but I think I'd been sent to bed early for some reason. I climbed out of my bedroom window, jumped the garden fence, and ran ten minutes down the road to my grandfather's house. I knocked on the door and, when he opened it, he found me in floods of tears. I told him that I hated my mother and father and was never going back home again.

From the outside, my grandfather's house was a nondescript red brick terrace with peeling paint on the windowsills and a dead plant in a pot beside the grubby white PVC front door. Once inside, however, it was as though you'd been transported to another time and place. Walls of dark, rich reds and greens with mahogany floors adorned with elaborate Persian rugs. In the front room the open fireplace, which always seemed far too grand for the size of the house, roared luxuriously no matter what time of year it was.

The man himself was a giant teddy bear with rosy-red cheeks and a resplendent bushy white moustache. He was one of those people who never seemed to have been young. When I was nine years old, he would still have had twenty years of good health ahead of him and would've still only been in his late sixties, yet he always looked exactly the same to me: a jolly old man with a heart as big as his belly. He wore a faded green cardigan with a white shirt underneath and baggy corduroy trousers. Again, I don't remember ever seeing him wearing anything else. Years later, after he'd passed away, Jen and I were clearing his belongings from the house. I remember how we were both overcome with a mixture of tears and laughter when we opened his wardrobe to discover rows of near-identical cardigans and white shirts. He was a constant for us; it was as though he'd been born fully formed as our grandfather.

He picked me up and carried me into the front room, where he sat me down on the sofa. I considered myself too old to be carried like a baby by this point in my life and certainly wouldn't have allowed my parents to scoop me up in this manner. But I never applied the same rules to my grandfather. Just as he never changed appearance in my eyes, I too was ageless in his presence. I was simply his grandson. He disappeared into the kitchen and returned moments later with a large bag of pink and white marshmallows and a glass of milk. As I knew he would. He always had marshmallows to give me no matter the situation and I would forever associate their look, smell, texture and taste with his generous smiling face.

When I had calmed and the tears had dried, he told me the story of how my mother had once run away from home when she was a young girl. He recalled how worried he was and how he had been about to call the police when he heard a noise coming from the direction of the garden shed. He went on to tell me how my mother had cried for hours and how he had held her in his arms until she eventually fell asleep, somehow making me feel as though I too wanted desperately to hold my mother now. To never ever make her cry. At the same time, he made it seem as though he and I were somehow co-conspirators, that this was a secret story between the two of us.

I too fell asleep in his arms that night and when I awoke the next morning, I was in my own bed at home. My parents

never mentioned me running away, as though my grandfather had somehow snuck me back into the house without
them ever realising that I'd gone. I never mentioned to my
mother the story of her running away to the garden shed
when she was young either. Years later it would strike me
that, had my grandfather not shared the story with me that
night all those years ago, it would no longer exist within
living memory. It would be gone forever, buried with the
layers. A memory of a memory of the dead.

The man's face is impossibly weathered; sallow and drained of life. He sits cross-legged, wrapped in blankets, with an upturned baseball cap on the pavement in front of him. He leans forward as if slowly falling, until his head nearly touches the ground, and then slowly pulls his body back up again. He keeps doing this, over and over, like a life-size perpetual motion figurine. He's silent and his eyes are rolling back into his head. As I sit and watch, endless streams of commuters blur past him without registering his presence. Two realities existing side by side but slightly out of sync, as if time is progressing at two different speeds. I find that I can zone in and out of both realities and observe the scene from either perspective. At one point a young girl, also wrapped in blankets and with a semi-dreadlocked mass of brown hair, emerges from the blur. She steps from one world into the other and sits beside him. She looks at him for a moment or two before picking up the cap from the pavement and emptying its contents into her hand. Then she slips away again, rejoining the mass of passing bodies, as if she'd never been there.

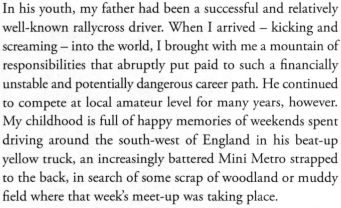

In his youth, my father had been a successful and relatively well-known rallycross driver. When I arrived – kicking and screaming – into the world, I brought with me a mountain of responsibilities that abruptly put paid to such a financially unstable and potentially dangerous career path. He continued to compete at local amateur level for many years, however. My childhood is full of happy memories of weekends spent driving around the south-west of England in his beat-up yellow truck, an increasingly battered Mini Metro strapped to the back, in search of some scrap of woodland or muddy field where that week's meet-up was taking place.

It was always something that just the two of us did together, father and son. I can still smell the petrol and burger vans through the mists of time. Vivid flash images of those days are burned into my consciousness forever. The cold and tatty interior of the truck, festooned with empty drink cans that rolled across the floor beneath my feet as it deafeningly spluttered and grumbled its way down bumpy dirt tracks. My father's giant hand wrapped around mine as he guided us through a bustling paddock area, the air so thick with dust that my eyes would sting for days afterwards. Roaring engines and indecipherable commentary booming from loudspeakers precariously strapped to hastily erected poles and fence posts. The heat that would emanate from my father as he stepped from the car and removed his helmet.

I remember on one occasion when I was about seven years old, the two of us were travelling to an event for the whole weekend and my father came to collect me from school on the Friday afternoon. He arrived early and walked into the school building to find me. He was carrying his crash helmet and dressed in his rallycross overalls, adorned with various colourful logos amid the oil stains. He approached my teacher and asked if I could leave early with him. As he did this, there were audible intakes of breath from the children around me as they turned to face me. One girl leaned towards me and whispered, 'Is that your dad?' I remember swelling with pride as I nodded my assent and the girl quietly exclaimed, 'Wow.' The teacher called me to the front of the class and wished us both luck for the weekend ahead. As I took my father's hand, I looked back at my classmates to see them all staring back at me in wide-eyed admiration. It was as though I'd just been collected from school by Superman. As we left the building, I looked up adoringly at my father and he looked down at me with a broad smile and winked.

■

The rain is falling hard now, and the street is deserted. I stand at the window and look at the figures inside. They move and converse with tired mundane purpose. Abstract yet so familiar I almost... The woman behind the counter smiles then stops smiling. Opens her mouth then closes it. Nods her head then shakes it again. She takes the goods, scans them and returns them one at a time. As one figure turns away from her, another sidles up to the counter and the whole scene is replayed. The scene is the void.

My breath is fogging the glass in front of my face now and the figures inside are fading from view. I try to feel the rain as it lashes down. To get some sense of it as it soaks through my clothes and hair. I turn from the window and walk along the empty pavement. The asphalt underneath my feet is cracked and old. A car speeds past with its headlights set to full beam and splashes my legs with dirty black puddle water. It's early evening and the world is blurred and murky. The rain is loud and violent but it masks an underlying dullness. There is no sun but I cannot see the clouds that obscure it. There is only grey. Only numbness.

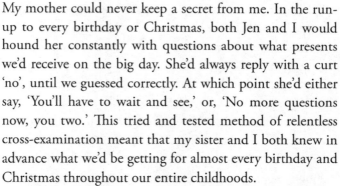

My mother could never keep a secret from me. In the run-up to every birthday or Christmas, both Jen and I would hound her constantly with questions about what presents we'd receive on the big day. She'd always reply with a curt 'no', until we guessed correctly. At which point she'd either say, 'You'll have to wait and see,' or, 'No more questions now, you two.' This tried and tested method of relentless cross-examination meant that my sister and I both knew in advance what we'd be getting for almost every birthday and Christmas throughout our entire childhoods.

Then, one year we both desperately wanted BMX bikes for Christmas and began badgering our parents from mid-September onwards. In early December we inevitably began our campaign of intimidation towards our mother. We constantly asked her if we'd be getting the bikes, in amongst other questions about smaller gifts from our ridiculously lengthy lists. My mother, to our shock and distress, resolutely replied in the negative. She'd give us the usual and telling 'wait and see' regarding the odd Care Bear or *Star Wars* toy, but when it came to the BMXs it was always a stern 'no'. As the day began to get worryingly close, the noes even became apologetic. 'Sorry you two, but we just can't afford it I'm afraid. Maybe next year.' We were devastated. By the time we sat under the tree on Christmas morning, we'd resigned ourselves to the fact that no BMXs would be forthcoming. We hadn't yet decided if we'd ever forgive our parents for this betrayal. After we'd unwrapped our presents and were busy stuffing our spoilt faces with chocolate, my mother announced casually that there might be two more presents for us waiting in the garden.

The thing that's stayed with me from that day is not the sheer joy that my sister and I both felt at receiving the bikes, but the look on my mother's face when we turned towards her once we'd realised what was happening. It wasn't a look of triumph that she'd finally managed to hoodwink us; there was no laughter or mock exasperation there. Her face glowed radiantly with a selfless happiness at the sight of our pleasure. I saw and felt the depth of her love for us at that moment. Once I recognised and understood that love, I'd see it emanating from her always. Whether through concern for me as she plastered up a grazed knee or through anger or disapproval when I misbehaved. I always knew that whatever life threw at me, there was someone who loved me, unconditionally and without question or pause. A love that was kind, protective, nurturing and fierce. To live life knowing that you are loved in that way is like being given a head start.

■

There is a wide doorway set back from the soot-black wall underneath the road bridge that seems to have its own unseen source of warmth. I sit there and wait for the sun to rise so that I can leave this place for somewhere – anywhere – different. This city that no longer knows me. The wall across the empty expanse of road from where I sit is covered in graffiti. Seemingly random words scrawled in bright colours from floor to ceiling. Aggressive single-syllable words. Blaze, shank and raid. A search for individuality that reads like an exhausted stereotype. In among the lost souls is the meticulously detailed image of a young girl's face with a single blood-red teardrop rolling down her cheek. A sound-less scream in the night from within the cold inevitability of it all. I hear a faint thud as bird shit lands on the pavement a few feet away from me. I look up to see that hundreds of silent pigeons are huddled together on the rafters above. Delicate docile birds made vermin by the filth of our ever-expanding endeavours. Their mangled and deformed feet cling to their peeling industrial perches. The sight of them tugs on something deep within me so that I almost… I see now that the pavement is covered in their excrement and I try to smell it through the smog and soot but cannot.

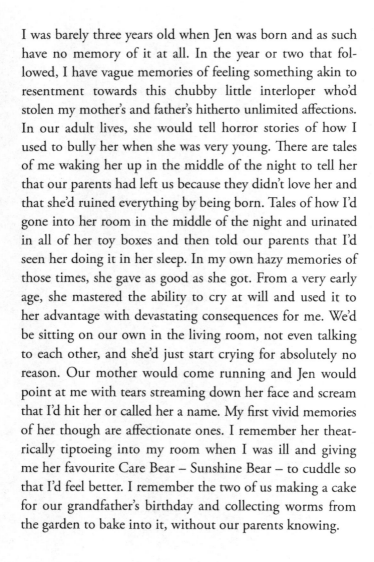

I was barely three years old when Jen was born and as such have no memory of it at all. In the year or two that followed, I have vague memories of feeling something akin to resentment towards this chubby little interloper who'd stolen my mother's and father's hitherto unlimited affections. In our adult lives, she would tell horror stories of how I used to bully her when she was very young. There are tales of me waking her up in the middle of the night to tell her that our parents had left us because they didn't love her and that she'd ruined everything by being born. Tales of how I'd gone into her room in the middle of the night and urinated in all of her toy boxes and then told our parents that I'd seen her doing it in her sleep. In my own hazy memories of those times, she gave as good as she got. From a very early age, she mastered the ability to cry at will and used it to her advantage with devastating consequences for me. We'd be sitting on our own in the living room, not even talking to each other, and she'd just start crying for absolutely no reason. Our mother would come running and Jen would point at me with tears streaming down her face and scream that I'd hit her or called her a name. My first vivid memories of her though are affectionate ones. I remember her theatrically tiptoeing into my room when I was ill and giving me her favourite Care Bear – Sunshine Bear – to cuddle so that I'd feel better. I remember the two of us making a cake for our grandfather's birthday and collecting worms from the garden to bake into it, without our parents knowing.

She was a cute mass of black curly hair who would grow up to become a strong and beautiful person. Despite me being older than her, she asserted herself as the dominant member of the partnership early on. In later life, people would regularly assume that she was the older sibling, which increasingly frustrated her. But she forged the role for herself and performed it well. Once when I was playing football at breaktime in primary school, I was hacked down by a boy in the year above me. I collapsed onto the floor in a heap, clutching my ankle where he had kicked me. I focused all of my energy into not bursting into tears in front of everyone and instead writhed around on the grass with gritted teeth as the pain slowly subsided. Jen and her friend had been sitting on the sidelines watching us play. When she saw what happened, she marched onto the pitch, went straight up to the older boy and kicked him in the crotch. He collapsed onto the ground beside me, wincing in agony, as everyone around us started laughing. My friends were scared of Jen from that day on and it would not be the last time that she stepped up to fight my corner for me.

■

They appear from the empty spaces like a whistling army of outcasts. Neon yellow uniforms blackened by the night. Their ramshackle carts rattle and clatter as their standard-issue broomsticks get to work. Sweep and scoop, sweep and scoop. A choreographed routine in the world's longest-running dystopian drama. An endless attempt to wash away the filth of disposable gluttony. The brightly packaged puke and the logo-laden landfill. And they whistle as they work. As money-makers stir in their satin sheets, they whistle. As the lonely gaze into the abyss of a new day, they whistle. As children scream and television screens flicker into life, as fat spits and treated water spews from showerhead to gutter, they whistle. Through discarded meat and broken glass, through till receipts and yesterday's news. Through gum and plastic-polyethylene and polystyrene and Styrofoam and polyester, polyamide and polypropylene. They whistle and then they vanish. Unseen and unconsidered. Imprisoned enablers. The darkness swallows them and then yields to the grey dawn light so that the meaningless march of excess may resume, unburdened by the whistling truth of the night.

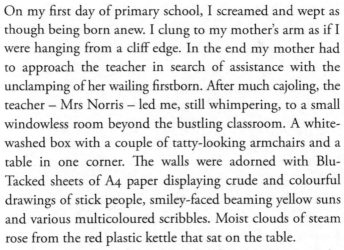

On my first day of primary school, I screamed and wept as though being born anew. I clung to my mother's arm as if I were hanging from a cliff edge. In the end my mother had to approach the teacher in search of assistance with the unclamping of her wailing firstborn. After much cajoling, the teacher – Mrs Norris – led me, still whimpering, to a small windowless room beyond the bustling classroom. A white-washed box with a couple of tatty-looking armchairs and a table in one corner. The walls were adorned with Blu-Tacked sheets of A4 paper displaying crude and colourful drawings of stick people, smiley-faced beaming yellow suns and various multicoloured scribbles. Moist clouds of steam rose from the red plastic kettle that sat on the table.

A boy sat in one of the chairs, his feet dangling over the edge, nowhere near to reaching the black-and-white chequered vinyl floor. His face was soaked with tears as snot bubbles shrank and expanded from his nose in time with his heavy, post-tantrum breathing. His hair was a wiry, unruly mass of wavy blonde. His untucked packet-fresh white shirt protruded from the bottom of his twisted oversized blue jumper. He looked up at me as we entered the room, his pale eyes surveying me before darting back to the floor.

'This is Roland,' said Mrs Norris, before following up the introduction with some calming collection of words long since lost to the mists of time. She sat me on the chair opposite the boy and left the room. A long silence followed as the two of us fought back the tears, weighing each other up. Eventually, as it became apparent that we had been abandoned, I spoke:

'My daddy is a racing driver.'

'No, he isn't!'

'Is!'

'Yeah, well, my daddy's the arm-wrestling world champion.'

'Wow!'

For the record, I can confirm with complete confidence that Rolly's dad wasn't the arm-wrestling world champion. I don't even think there is an arm-wrestling world champion. But, by the time Mrs Norris had re-entered the room, we had become the best of friends. A friendship that would endure the next three decades. In primary school we would be inseparable, in secondary school we'd be part of the same gang and at university we'd be housemates. We'd get drunk for the first time together, smoke our first cigarette together and lose our respective virginities in the same year. I would be Rolly's best man at his wedding and he would be the first person I came out to in my teens.

'Can you tell me your name?'
  'Where is the pain?'
  'Can you feel this?'
  'Squeeze my hand for me.'

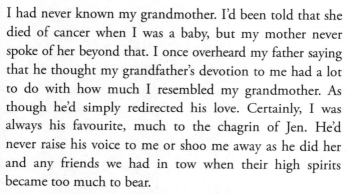

I had never known my grandmother. I'd been told that she died of cancer when I was a baby, but my mother never spoke of her beyond that. I once overheard my father saying that he thought my grandfather's devotion to me had a lot to do with how much I resembled my grandmother. As though he'd simply redirected his love. Certainly, I was always his favourite, much to the chagrin of Jen. He'd never raise his voice to me or shoo me away as he did her and any friends we had in tow when their high spirits became too much to bear.

I must've been ten years old before I began to think it odd that nobody ever spoke of my grandmother. I remember asking my parents about it and being met with very obvious attempts at deflection. I was at my grandfather's house a few days after I'd asked them, scoffing marshmallows as he read to me. He'd always read me stories. We'd gone through AA Milne and Enid Blyton and were currently working our way through *Stig of the Dump*. I interrupted him to ask why there were no pictures of my grandmother anywhere in his house. We had one photograph in our house, hidden away in the spare room. The two of them arm in arm at someone's wedding. But it was blurred and grainy and I couldn't really make out what she actually looked like.

I knew immediately that my words had shocked him. He stopped and looked up at me, a flash of something I'd never seen before, maybe anger, then almost immediately something worse. There were tears in his eyes. I'd never seen a grown-up cry before. Apart from my mother, but that didn't count because she cried when she was happy, which at the time I thought probably meant she was mad. But my grandfather wasn't happy, I don't think. I felt a million things I couldn't make sense of. Guilt, embarrassment, but mainly fear.

'As it happens,' he said, breaking into a strange smile as a tear ran down his rosy cheek, 'there are lots of pictures of your grandmother in this house. Would you like to see them?'

He led me up the stairs and into his bedroom. I'd only been in there once or twice before and it had seemed so much bigger on those occasions. He produced an old-fashioned silver key from his pocket, walked across the room and bent down to unlock a large drawer at the bottom of the ornate wardrobe that filled one corner of the room.

The drawer was lined in a warm orange colour and the air around it was thick with the smell of perfume. It was full to the brim with photographs. Some loose, some in albums, some framed. She stared up at us with a variety of different expressions. Smiling, straight-faced, laughing, young, middle-aged, in love. A handsome woman with my eyes and my mother's smile. As my grandfather picked up and opened one of the albums, I looked up at him to find him smiling down at me.

'She was a wonderful woman. She would have loved you. You would've been her golden boy.'

Over the next hour or so, we sat in his bedroom as he talked me through the photographs and the memories they evoked in him. I learnt some of the truth about my grandmother. That she had left him just before my mother and father were married. She'd run off without any explanation and never attempted to make contact again. It was true that she had died of cancer when I was a baby. But he found this out only when he was contacted by a solicitor over the phone. She'd left him her life savings in her will. He gently did his best to explain that my mother had never forgiven her for leaving them and that he didn't feel able to put up photographs around the house for fear of upsetting her.

Even as it was happening, I sensed that this was a one-time thing. He was allowing me to see him like this and to share in his secret. But only me, and only once. He did briefly attempt to explain to me that my parents and everyone else had assumed he'd removed all trace of the love of his life so that he could move on. He suspected they never spoke of her because he never spoke of her. They were respecting his decision to leave her in the past, to block out the pain of it all. It was my first experience of grief. Its all-consuming control. Its ability to change people, to break them. But he wasn't broken, not really. He needed this locked-away secret so he could spend time with her. That's all.

He never actually told me to keep the drawer a secret, or indeed that only the two of us knew of its existence. But he didn't need to. Sure enough, years later, after he'd passed away, the family was shocked and horrified upon discovering the drawer. I pretended to be as surprised as everyone else, but I think Jen twigged the truth of it.

The lights are always on here, burning endlessly and illuminating the vast space, almost lifeless in the gasping embers of night. A man scours the concrete floors for discarded fag ends, pausing intermittently to frantically rub his eyes with the heels of his hands. As though if he rubs hard enough, he may suddenly awake from this. A faint smell of stale ammonia permeates the air. Empty escalators glide up and down in senseless synchronicity as a rat scurries through the shadows. I hear the first train arriving and walk through the open barriers towards it. A bleary-eyed guard, still at home with his wife and cornflakes, stares through me, unseeing. I wonder if he understands it could all disappear in an instant. If he is grateful for the things he has. The ordinary things. Is there something like anger then?

The seats are covered with the dead skin of yesterday's ashen-faced commuters. As I sit down, their dust cloud envelopes me. The city fades from view. The screech and grinding of the train blasts through the suburbs. Rows and rows and rows. Brick and lawn, lawn and brick. We stop at empty stations and wait in silence for no one. Or maybe not. Perhaps they are all around me, staring and not staring. Resigned to the day ahead. Boarding and alighting, alighting and boarding. Rows and rows and rows.

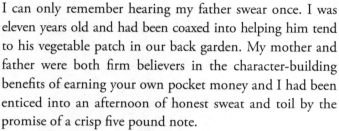

I can only remember hearing my father swear once. I was eleven years old and had been coaxed into helping him tend to his vegetable patch in our back garden. My mother and father were both firm believers in the character-building benefits of earning your own pocket money and I had been enticed into an afternoon of honest sweat and toil by the promise of a crisp five pound note.

I inherited many of my father's character traits and shared in many of his interests, but green fingers were not among them. My eleven-year-old self could think of no less appealing way to spend my precious weekend hours, but my father revelled in the mud and simplicity of it all. He was an outdoorsman in every sense. A physically strong and broad-shouldered man for whom the idea of working in an office would have seemed akin to a term of imprisonment. In truth, I was of no help whatsoever to him. My role was primarily to hold things. Things which could just as easily have sat on the ground and then been passed to him when he asked for them. It was a cold and grey afternoon but he was dressed, as ever, in a cotton shirt with the sleeves rolled up and a pair of old trousers bearing the mud and oil stains of productive days gone by. He wiped the sweat from his brow as I stood still and shivered in the drizzling rain. I wore a dark-blue parka coat two sizes too big for me and a pair of bright-red goalkeeping gloves. I begrudgingly clutched a bag of seeds in one hand and a bulb of some description in the other.

He picked up a large garden fork the size of a shovel and drove it into the soil with all of his considerable strength. Then he froze mid-action as though time had stopped. It took me a few seconds to understand what I was seeing. The fork had gone straight through his foot and into the mud beneath. A few more seconds passed in frozen silence. I looked up at him, then back at the ground. I did this several times, my eyes wide and my mouth hanging open in disbelief. Finally, he looked at me. His face was red but he wore the furrowed expression of a man pondering a tricky crossword clue. In a calm but strained voice that I'd never heard him use before he spoke: 'Go indoors and get your fucking mother.'

I ran like the wind. Even in my panic to reach my mother, I remember being stunned – almost giddy with shock – at hearing my father use the F-word. My mother insisted that he didn't remove the fork from his foot as she'd read somewhere that this could cause further loss of blood. So, as we drove to the hospital and then sat in A&E waiting to be seen by a doctor, my father still had the large garden fork protruding from his wellington boot.

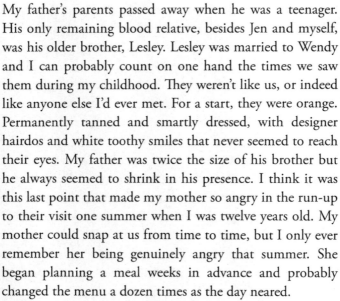

My father's parents passed away when he was a teenager. His only remaining blood relative, besides Jen and myself, was his older brother, Lesley. Lesley was married to Wendy and I can probably count on one hand the times we saw them during my childhood. They weren't like us, or indeed like anyone else I'd ever met. For a start, they were orange. Permanently tanned and smartly dressed, with designer hairdos and white toothy smiles that never seemed to reach their eyes. My father was twice the size of his brother but he always seemed to shrink in his presence. I think it was this last point that made my mother so angry in the run-up to their visit one summer when I was twelve years old. My mother could snap at us from time to time, but I only ever remember her being genuinely angry that summer. She began planning a meal weeks in advance and probably changed the menu a dozen times as the day neared.

Usually, when my mother became worried or anxious about something, my father would be able to calm her. The reverse was also true. If my father lost his temper for any reason, my mother was always able to reach him when others could not. They always seemed somehow able to ground each other. On this occasion, however, I recall my father being noticeably absent. He appeared to spend most of his time in the weeks that preceded his brother's visit digging holes in the garden or 'sorting things out' in the loft. Jen would later tell me that on the day before they arrived, she saw him sitting in the car out on the road, the engine switched off, gazing lifelessly into the distance.

When the day finally arrived, my grandfather was called in for moral support. My mother had cooked a Sunday roast with all the trimmings and had requested that he bring with him a jar of his famous homemade pickled red cabbage. I had been visiting my grandfather when she made the call a few days earlier and remember him holding the phone comically far away from his ear and wincing as my mother bellowed her response to his observation that a Sunday roast had been an unusual choice for a sweltering midsummer day. So too were the matching itchy maroon jumpers that Jen and I were forced into on the morning of the big day. My father looked even more uncomfortable than either of us in his shirt and tie. My grandfather had trimmed his bushy moustache and my mother wore a long and flowing navy-blue dress. In short, my family had made every effort to look like someone else's family.

Lesley and Wendy arrived in matching sunglasses and jaundiced complexions. They had recently returned from a holiday in the US and came bearing gifts. I received a Miami Dolphins football shirt that would later take up residence in my father's workshop, reborn as an oily rag. Jen was presented with a garish bejewelled silver necklace that bore the name 'Jan'. My mother was given a charcoal face mask and my father a T-shirt that read 'My brother went to Florida and all I got was this lousy T-shirt'. The first half an hour or so passed without incident as we all sat and listened to tales of their trip stateside. Even as a twelve-year-old, I noticed that at no point did either Lesley or Wendy ask my parents or grandfather how they were or what they'd been up to. Indeed, I don't think any of my family actually said a word, simply nodding and smiling and occasionally chuckling when it seemed appropriate to do so.

Things started to become tense as soon as we'd all sat at the table for dinner. My mother offered round the various dishes of potatoes, sprouts, Yorkshire puddings and such as my grandfather sliced up the joint of meat. Wendy ate two sprouts, a slice of carrot and half a parsnip. She and Lesley exchanged unpleasant knowing glances throughout and at one stage she offered up the opinion that a roast dinner was an unusual choice for a sweltering midsummer day. And then there were Lesley's belittling comments towards my father. He would start sentences with things like, 'Of course, my brother never was much of a thinker' or, 'Mind you, Mother and Father never held out much hope.' My father would sit looking uncomfortable throughout, sheepishly staring down at his food.

Just as it did my mother, seeing him like this made me angry. My father was the strongest man I knew. Not just physically either. His strength of character was something I was always in awe of. He would stand up and speak out for the things he believed in and, in particular, for his family. Both he and my mother were our fierce protectors. But there was this blind spot where his brother was concerned. As though Lesley's very presence rendered him weak, somehow lesser. It seemed as though it were a different man sat hunched over his dinner plate. A stranger. I never found out what the original cause of the brothers' animosity had been. In later years, my mother hinted that Lesley had at some point lent my father money and subsequently never let him forget it, but any further details were not forthcoming.

I remember this particular visit above any other because it was the last. It was the final time in my life that I would ever see my father cowed in this manner. Although I would see my uncle and aunt again, they would never again visit our house. At some point, just as Lesley was commenting on how ill-suited my father was to smart attire, my mother stood up.

'I think you've said enough.'

There was a brief silence before Lesley, with a smug grin on his orange face, lent back on his chair and replied, 'I beg your pardon?'

'I will not sit here a moment longer and listen to you belittling my husband and my family.'

She was a lioness that day, fighting for her pride.

Lesley looked at my father, who sat staring, slack-jawed, at my mother. 'I think your wife has taken leave of her senses.'

Another silence.

My father slowly took his eyes from my mother and turned to face his brother. Then he stood up. 'Get out. Both of you.'

Then my grandfather stood up. Then I stood up. Then Jen. Wendy turned from orange to a maroon that exactly matched my jumper. Lesley tried to maintain the smug grin, but his eyes gave him away.

The following few moments were some of the strangest, most awkward and exciting of my entire life up to that point. Lesley was muttering words like 'ridiculous', 'pathetic' and 'outraged' as the two of them shuffled crestfallen from the house.

Just before my father shut the door in his brother's face, Jen called out, 'And my name is Jen! With an E ... Idiots!'

Once he'd shut the door, my father turned and walked purposefully towards my mother. They embraced and kissed. My grandfather turned to Jen and I and mimed being sick. The evening that followed was one that the five of us would remember and talk about always. My father roared with laughter as Jen did po-faced impressions of Wendy eating a parsnip. My grandfather welled up as he told my mother how proud of her he was. We ate mountains of food and all agreed that roast dinners tasted a million times better in the sweltering heat of summer. I caught my mother's eye as she looked lovingly at her pride.

The off-white coffee cup is chipped and dirt-blackened veins spread across its surface like a cancer. The air is thick with frying flesh and chip fat. An overweight middle-aged man with sweaty, hairy hands passes a plate piled with food to a pallid, coughing man carrying a folded newspaper with a headline reading: 'Benefit-collecting immigrants given free homes scandal.' A woman on the table next to mine slurps her tea and tuts loudly at an empty chair. The light overhead flickers and for a second the scene dissolves. Like losing radio reception under a road bridge. Ants scurry across a corner of the yellow Formica tabletop and I see that my fingernails are long and black with dirt. I sip the beige, bitter liquid and feel it cascade down my throat. I can't tell if it's burning me or not. This realisation fades into another. That I may be lost in the void forever now. Something like panic briefly bubbles up and I almost... Outside the breath-misted windows, ethereal figures slither in a blur of colours and smoke.

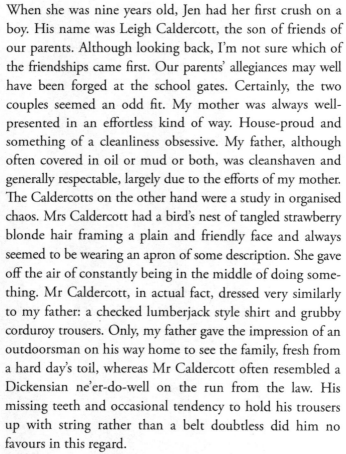

When she was nine years old, Jen had her first crush on a boy. His name was Leigh Caldercott, the son of friends of our parents. Although looking back, I'm not sure which of the friendships came first. Our parents' allegiances may well have been forged at the school gates. Certainly, the two couples seemed an odd fit. My mother was always well-presented in an effortless kind of way. House-proud and something of a cleanliness obsessive. My father, although often covered in oil or mud or both, was cleanshaven and generally respectable, largely due to the efforts of my mother. The Caldercotts on the other hand were a study in organised chaos. Mrs Caldercott had a bird's nest of tangled strawberry blonde hair framing a plain and friendly face and always seemed to be wearing an apron of some description. She gave off the air of constantly being in the middle of doing something. Mr Caldercott, in actual fact, dressed very similarly to my father: a checked lumberjack style shirt and grubby corduroy trousers. Only, my father gave the impression of an outdoorsman on his way home to see the family, fresh from a hard day's toil, whereas Mr Caldercott often resembled a Dickensian ne'er-do-well on the run from the law. His missing teeth and occasional tendency to hold his trousers up with string rather than a belt doubtless did him no favours in this regard.

I remember on one occasion the whole Caldercott clan came to visit for the afternoon. Mr Caldercott and my father sat on the sofa watching the rugby while I sat at the coffee table in front of them drawing a picture of Optimus Prime. My mother, Mrs Caldercott, Jen and Leigh all sat around the table in the dining room playing cards while the radio in the background counted down the Top 40. The afternoon was a pleasant one with easy-flowing conversations. If anything of note occurred then it has long since faded from my memory. Eventually the time came for the Caldercotts to say their goodbyes. A short while after they'd gone, Jen and I walked into the living room to find my mother removing the sofa cushions where Mr Caldercott had been sitting.

'What are you doing, Mum?' asked Jen.

'Oh, nothing. Just time these old things went in the wash is all.'

We looked at our father, who was trying and failing to hold back a laugh. 'Your mother thinks Mr Caldercott may have a few personal hygiene problems.'

'Now that's not true, you just keep your gob shut thanks very much,' said my mother.

'What do you mean?' I asked.

'Never you mind, it's nothing. Your father's just being silly.'

We looked again at our father and he pinched his nose at us and mimed fanning the air in front of his face. My mother gave him a playful slap on her way out of the room, but she was smiling as she did so.

Leigh himself had a wiry, wily appearance. Taller than average with small, darting, dark-blue eyes and a wavy mop of unruly mousy brown hair. He and Jen seemed to get on like a house on fire. They'd play together in the evenings after school and were regulars at each other's dinner tables throughout the week. I'd occasionally try and tease her about it but, much to my disappointment, she wasn't in the slightest bit embarrassed. Quite the opposite in fact.

One day on the school playground, Jen got into an argument with a group of friends who didn't believe her when she claimed to have a secret boyfriend. She stormed over to where Leigh was standing with some of his schoolmates, grabbed him by the arm, pulled him across the playground and presented him like a trophy to her friends. With her chin jutting defiantly outwards, she loudly and proudly declared, 'This is my boyfriend, Leigh, and we're in love.'

Her friends collapsed into fits of giggles, which was nothing compared to the guffaws emanating from Leigh's friends as they pointed at him and bent double with laughter. Leigh looked utterly mortified, immediately turned bright red and appeared to be on the verge of tears.

'Liar!' he said. 'I'm not your boyfriend … You're ugly.'

News of the encounter quickly and remorselessly spread throughout the school. When Rolly and I heard about what had happened, we both agreed that, when all is said and done, Leigh really had no other option than to react in the way he did. Girls had fleas, after all. We concluded that, in his shoes, we'd have done exactly the same thing. We still fell about laughing though, it goes without saying. In typically selfish older brother fashion, I hadn't even considered how the events of the day would have affected Jen. She was devastated. When my mother picked us up from school, Jen was in tears. Tears that persisted throughout the journey home and well into the evening. She refused to tell my mother what had happened but, although my own lips remained sealed in a show of solidarity, she found out soon enough. In that way that mothers do, she had somehow known who to call and, once off the phone with Mrs Caldercott, she stopped asking Jen what was wrong and instead sat quietly beside her on the sofa stroking her hair.

A week or so later, my mother and Mrs Caldercott had devised a day trip for us all in an attempt to resolve the situation and get Jen and Leigh talking again. The ultimate destination escapes me now, but it is of no consequence because we never got there. Mrs Caldercott was driving us all in her rust-coloured estate, with my mother in the passenger seat and Jen, Leigh and I in the back. I was in the middle of the stony silent trio, feeling as uncomfortable as I'd ever felt in all of my eleven years. Mrs Caldercott regularly glanced at us all in her rear-view mirror, her brow creased into a frown. In the end she attempted to break the deadlock.

'Who wants to stop for an ice cream?'

I raised my hand enthusiastically, Leigh nodded sullenly and Jen suddenly looked to be on the brink of tears.

'Well I'd better not have one as I'm so fat and ugly,' she muttered, scowling at Leigh.

'I said you were ugly, not fat!'

'Leigh!' came the unified cry from the front seats.

'Well I may be ugly but at least I'm not smelly!'

'I don't smell!' barked Leigh.

'You do. Your family is so smelly that my mum has to wash our sofa every time you come round our house!'

'Jen! Don't be so silly, you know that's not true!'

But it was too late. My mother had turned bright red and protested far too vehemently. For my part, I didn't help matters much by first staring in panic at my mother and then breaking into a nervous giggle. My mother looked imploringly at Mrs Caldercott but her eyes remained on the road. The inhabitants of the back seat continued to squabble and exchange insults until the oversized wagon arrived back on our driveway. The stony silence had transferred to the front of the car.

We didn't see much of the Caldercotts after that. No more house visits or shared meals. I don't remember Jen being in trouble for what had happened. Everyone just seemed upset and separate for a while. Then over time this faded as we all got on with our lives. Nobody mentioned what had happened for many years until, at some point a decade or so later, the whole episode became an amusing anecdote. Time had turned the memory into something that united us. A blunt-edged and comical chapter in our combined story.

■

The windows are boarded up and daubed in spray paint. Shoots of green emerge from the cracks in the concrete forecourt as if the earth may yet erase our flatpack tenements and crumbling temples of industry. The ghosts of decades of skilled and unskilled corpses make no sound through the darkness. Their work has ceased and the product of their labour been forgotten. Entire lives played out in the bustling spaces now rendered vacant ruins. There are no screams from the beyond, no distant laughter or whirl of machinery. Mothers, fathers, drunkards and poets. The average and the lost, the bright and the submissive. Scandals and fish suppers. Hope and haberdashery. They are gone. But I feel them, don't I? I lament them. That's something, isn't it? A feeling. In their wake? A shell. A blemish awaiting the inevitable.

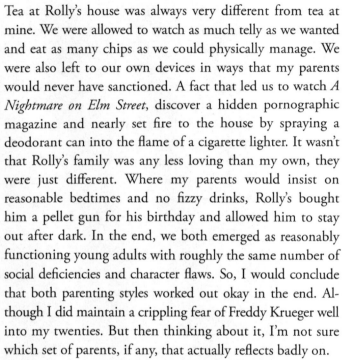

Tea at Rolly's house was always very different from tea at mine. We were allowed to watch as much telly as we wanted and eat as many chips as we could physically manage. We were also left to our own devices in ways that my parents would never have sanctioned. A fact that led us to watch *A Nightmare on Elm Street*, discover a hidden pornographic magazine and nearly set fire to the house by spraying a deodorant can into the flame of a cigarette lighter. It wasn't that Rolly's family was any less loving than my own, they were just different. Where my parents would insist on reasonable bedtimes and no fizzy drinks, Rolly's bought him a pellet gun for his birthday and allowed him to stay out after dark. In the end, we both emerged as reasonably functioning young adults with roughly the same number of social deficiencies and character flaws. So, I would conclude that both parenting styles worked out okay in the end. Although I did maintain a crippling fear of Freddy Krueger well into my twenties. But then thinking about it, I'm not sure which set of parents, if any, that actually reflects badly on.

I have many happy memories of evenings spent in their home … and a few traumatic ones as well. Like the time I accidently walked dog poo all through the house. Or when I shot the next-door neighbour in the head. Rolly had told me that his mum had caught the boy next door, a sour-faced child a few years our junior, throwing stones at their beloved and elderly cat, Moo-Moo. She duly reprimanded him with considerable gusto and ensured that his parents punished him suitably as well. Nevertheless, Rolly and I felt that he had a bit more coming to him.

We loaded up the pellet gun and patiently waited at Rolly's bedroom window, like the lone gunman at the book depository in Dallas, Texas a few decades earlier. The window overlooked the lane at the rear of the houses where the boy would regularly ride his bike. Sure enough, after a while he appeared, pulling wheelies and making motorbike engine noises. Rolly lifted the gun to his shoulder and took aim.

'Actually, I don't think we should. What if it kills him?' he said, looking nervous and apologetic.

'Don't be a wimp, give it here.'

I took the gun, aimed and fired. In a one-off fluke of a shot that I doubt I'd be able to repeat if I had a hundred years to do so, I shot him clean in the forehead. He yelped and fell off his bike. He looked up at the window, where we both stood staring slack-jawed in disbelief. Then he screamed with tears and ran away clutching his face.

'Oh shit,' I said.

'Oh shit,' said Rolly.

Within the hour, we were standing in front of Rolly's mum as she glared down at us with a face full of fury.

'Which one of you did it?!'

We looked at each other in silence. Then I turned to face her and just as I opened my mouth to speak, Rolly interrupted.

'It was me,' he said. Then defiantly added, 'He had it coming, Mum. It was for Moo-Moo.'

'You bloody idiot, Rolly. You could have blinded him! Do you have any idea how much trouble you're in?'

Over the years, Rolly and I would go on to help each other out of trouble many times. But I never forgot that evening. How terrified I'd been as we waited to be discovered. How unbelievably relieved I felt to escape punishment. A relief that soon turned into a potent mixture of guilt and gratitude. The truth did eventually come out, as it happens. I finally confessed to a room of over one hundred people as I delivered my best man's speech at Rolly's wedding. It got a laugh.

✕

'Unknown Caucasian male between thirty-five and forty-five. Admitted with multiple headwounds, rib fractures and bruising to torso and legs.'

'Meaning … in simple terms?'

'He was beaten up.'

'Prognosis?'

'In simple terms?'

'Ha, if you don't mind.'

'He's out of danger and lucid. Won't be going anywhere for a few weeks.'

'He's said nothing at all?'

'No. No identification whatsoever.'

'Homeless?'

'Possibly, although if so, probably only recently based on general condition.'

'Okay, so I'll just run through everything I've got. See if anything causes a reaction.'

'I'll leave you to it.'

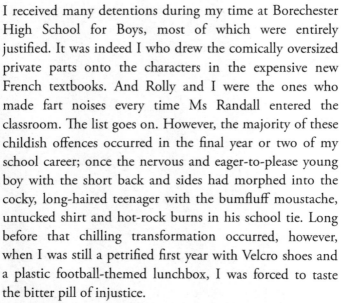

I received many detentions during my time at Borechester High School for Boys, most of which were entirely justified. It was indeed I who drew the comically oversized private parts onto the characters in the expensive new French textbooks. And Rolly and I were the ones who made fart noises every time Ms Randall entered the classroom. The list goes on. However, the majority of these childish offences occurred in the final year or two of my school career; once the nervous and eager-to-please young boy with the short back and sides had morphed into the cocky, long-haired teenager with the bumfluff moustache, untucked shirt and hot-rock burns in his school tie. Long before that chilling transformation occurred, however, when I was still a petrified first year with Velcro shoes and a plastic football-themed lunchbox, I was forced to taste the bitter pill of injustice.

Nigel Timkins was a short, skinny boy whose clothes were several sizes too big for him. He spoke with a pronounced lisp and sported a pudding basin haircut, clearly maintained by Mother Timkins. What chance did Nigel Timkins really ever have? He was, of course, an absolute godsend for the rest of us. Why would any potential bully waste their time on anyone else when there was Nigel to play with? On this occasion, an unruly group of boys in my class had – not for the first time – decided to hang the unfortunate Nigel Timkins by his feet from a third-floor classroom window, taking delight in his desperate screams.

That day I'd had the bad luck of walking past that specific classroom, likely on my way to fetch my beloved lunchbox from my locker along the same corridor. Attention caught by the wailing coming from the room, I poked my head round the door and watched in shock as Nigel was pulled back into the classroom. This was the day that Nigel – in a rare moment of defiance – decided that he'd had enough. As soon as his feet were planted on solid ground, he sprinted past me and out of the classroom, straight to the headmaster's office, where he blabbed the whole sorry tale including a list of perpetrators. A list that inexplicably included yours truly. That a forty-five-minute after-school detention was not an appropriate punishment for hanging a sobbing child from a third-floor window by his feet did not occur to me at the time. Neither did the fact that standing silently by as a scared little boy was viciously bullied meant that I probably deserved a good deal worse than the punishment I'd been given. I was consumed with the outrage of the wrongly accused.

I protested my innocence to teachers and parents alike. To my horror neither believed me and I was branded a bully.

One person did take me on my word though.

'If you say you didn't do it, then you didn't do it,' proclaimed my grandfather with gusto, as he handed me a bowl of pink and white marshmallows. My mother had phoned him to say that I wouldn't be visiting that evening as I'd been grounded due to the events of the day. My grandfather had taken it upon himself to immediately march round to our house and hear my side of the story. We were sitting at the kitchen table with Jen, my mother and my father.

'Oh, Dad, please! I was on the phone to the headmaster for nearly thirty minutes. He assured me there'd been no mistake. That poor boy,' retorted my mother as she glared at me across the table.

'Well now, I for one believe him. I'm no stranger to injustice myself, you know. Did I ever tell you the story of the laxative chocolate?'

At my grandfather's mention of this, my mother rolled her eyes and got up from the table. She was muttering something about it being the hundredth time she'd heard it as she walked away.

'No,' said Jen and I in unison.

'Well then. When I was a boy, no more than a year or two younger than you are now, you used to be able to buy these big chocolate bars that worked as laxatives.'

'What's a laxative?' asked Jen.

'What's that? Oh, erm, well, it's a…'

'It makes you need a poo,' I interjected. Jen nearly choked on her marshmallow as she descended into a fit of giggles.

'Well yes, exactly. Anyway, when I was a boy my parents were best friends with a family named the Fowlers. They had a boy my age by the name of Billy. We were friends, sort of. Friends in that way you are when your parents plonk the two of you together for days on end and leave you to get on with it. Billy was a naughty lad, led me astray on many an occasion … Anyway, this one time, my parents and I went around the Fowlers for the day. When we arrived in the morning, I spotted a big bar of chocolate on the dining table.' He chuckled to himself, momentarily lost in the memory, before carrying on. 'I remember that our old mutt Trigger spotted it too. He went and sat himself right underneath it, staring up at it. Ah, good old Trigger. Do you know he once saved me from a billy goat?'

'Yes!' we both exclaimed as one.

'Right you are. Anyway, Mr Fowler clocked me staring at the thing and told me not to go anywhere near it. It wasn't normal chocolate he said. I didn't think any more of it until after lunch. "Where's my chocolate?" Mr Fowler bellowed. He was a big chap. Arms like tree trunks. One big eyebrow … Anyway, to cut a long story short, Billy told him I'd eaten it! I protested, of course, but he didn't believe me. I knew Billy had eaten it because we were playing in the garden all morning and he disappeared at one point and when he came back, he had it all over his face. I'd told him to wipe it off before anyone saw it. He was a naughty lad, Billy. Anyway, Mr Fowler went and told Mrs Fowler and my parents that I'd pinched it. In no time at all I found myself surrounded by the lot of them, pointing their fingers and telling me not to be a little thief. My own parents! I was told I'd get no tea. And sure enough, later that afternoon we're all sitting in the front room and everyone's munching crumpets and tea cakes except me. I was starving but I was so angry that I didn't want to give them the satisfaction of whining. Of course, that's when it happened.'

He paused and gave us all a broad smile from beneath the bushy white moustache.

'What happened?!' I implored.

'Billy farted.'

We all laughed.

'Then he farted again. Then he … well, then he did more than fart. Everyone turned to stare at him as he let out a moan and ran from the room clutching his backside.'

'He pooed his pants!' said Jen delightedly.

'You're too right he did!' my grandfather said, chuckling between words.

I never confronted Nigel to ask why he'd added my name

to the list. Perhaps on some level I felt that I deserved it for never speaking up in his defence. Or perhaps that's giving my younger self far too much credit. More likely I didn't want to be seen talking to him.

■

The man paces up and down the pavement in front of the shining glass veneer of the high-rise building. His tailored pinstripe suit is protected from the falling rain by the overhanging ledge above his clay-puttied bedhead hairstyle. He drags hard on the cigarette in his long-fingered hand and inhales as though he's been waiting for this moment all day. He checks his gleaming gold wristwatch and swears under his breath. His pointed and heeled leather shoes clip clop as he paces back and forth. His phone rings out with a piercing generic clarity. His voice booms across the distance that separates us in a spewing stream of expletive-laden sneers and guttural belly laughs. An elderly woman approaches him with an arthritic hand held out in forlorn acceptance. He frowns disgustedly at her and silently mouths, 'Fuck off'. As she hobbles away, he flicks his cigarette to the ground, where it smoulders and dies amid a blueish plume of dancing toxic smoke. He checks his hair in the mirrored window before disappearing through the revolving doors.

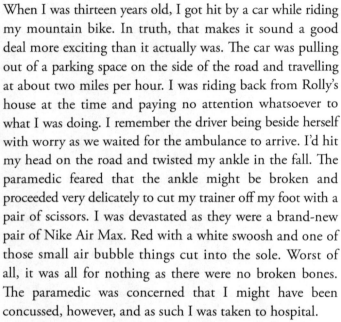

When I was thirteen years old, I got hit by a car while riding my mountain bike. In truth, that makes it sound a good deal more exciting than it actually was. The car was pulling out of a parking space on the side of the road and travelling at about two miles per hour. I was riding back from Rolly's house at the time and paying no attention whatsoever to what I was doing. I remember the driver being beside herself with worry as we waited for the ambulance to arrive. I'd hit my head on the road and twisted my ankle in the fall. The paramedic feared that the ankle might be broken and proceeded very delicately to cut my trainer off my foot with a pair of scissors. I was devastated as they were a brand-new pair of Nike Air Max. Red with a white swoosh and one of those small air bubble things cut into the sole. Worst of all, it was all for nothing as there were no broken bones. The paramedic was concerned that I might have been concussed, however, and as such I was taken to hospital.

Shortly after I got there, my parents, Jen and my grandfather all arrived. It soon became apparent that the injury wasn't serious, a hairline skull fracture. Although I do remember thinking that that sounded pretty serious to me. I would need to spend the night there so they could keep an eye on me and ensure that I didn't slip into a coma. This involved waking me up on the hour, every hour, throughout the night and shining a torch in my eyes. Once it was clear that I was in no real danger, my father took Jen and my grandfather home, while my mother stayed with me.

She sat by my bedside watching me like a hawk as I ate a hospital dinner of pie and chips, her eyes constantly scanning me for any signs that my head might be about to fall off and crack open. During the evening she found a tattered copy of *The Secret Diary of Adrian Mole Aged 13 and ¾* on the ward's reading shelf. She read it aloud to me as I lay in bed, just as she used to read to me when I was a young child. An obstinate pubescent part of me wanted to tell her that I was too old for bedtime stories, but I didn't because I knew that it wasn't true. I knew that my mum reading me a bedtime story was exactly what I wanted at that moment. I also didn't mention that I knew she was skipping over the rude bits in the book as I'd already read it, having borrowed it from Rolly earlier that year.

My mother didn't sleep a wink that night. I know this to be true because every time the nurse woke me up to shine a torch in my eyes, there she was. Standing beside him, wide awake and looking worried. My anxious guardian angel. The next morning the doctor said I was fine and free to go home. As he delivered the news, I watched my mother breathe a sigh of relief, her entire posture changing as the tension released. After he'd gone, she gave me a hug of bear-like intensity. It was as though she'd been scared to do so for the last twelve hours in case it put me into a coma. For a second, I thought it might as I struggled to breathe and squirmed in her arms in a bid for freedom.

I didn't get any replacement red Nike Air Max trainers with a white swoosh on. But I did get a shiny red cycling helmet that I was never allowed to leave the house without and that made me look like a plastic toadstool.

≡

By the time I was in my mid-teens, my father had all but given up the rallycross. A mixture of aching bones and financial restraints were the primary reasons for this, but there was another. For as long as I can remember, he and I would travel to the local meet-ups together. A father and son bonding ritual that meant our relationship remained close and one of mutual respect and understanding. For my father, a kind and loving man who wasn't always able to display his affections physically or verbally, those trips provided a crucial means of expressing his love for his son. A shared space wherein he could impart wisdom, provide parental guidance and keep in touch with the developing character of his firstborn. In subsequent years, he and Jen would establish a similar bond through their mutual interest in growing vegetables on their respective plots.

For me, as a child and early teenager, the adventures with my father were far more simplistic in their meaning and devoid of the weighty nuances that made them so significant for him. He was my childhood hero. I wanted to be like him and to be with him. I never really noticed or acknowledged that he had a paid profession on weekdays. To me, he was a racing driver. My friends from school had fathers who wore suits and sat in front of the television to watch the football at weekends. My father raced cars and was always covered in mud or oil. Once, when I must have been about ten years old, he was in a huge crash that would result in the Mini Metro being out of action for many months. I watched on in terror as people crowded around his stricken car. As he walked away supported by members of the St John Ambulance brigade, I ran towards him with tears streaming down my face, frantically pushing my way through the crowds. When he saw me, he smiled broadly and cheerfully called out, 'There's my boy. That was a good one, eh?'

He had broken his arm in several places but he never winced or showed any sign of pain. Not as the St John Ambulance woman manoeuvred the arm into a sling, nor as we travelled down the bumpy lanes and roads to the hospital in the back of his friend's van. Instead, he laughed and joked and had his good arm wrapped around me the whole time, only caring for my wellbeing and doing everything he could to ensure that I didn't worry.

Then, on one occasion when I was fourteen years old, I told him that I didn't want to go with him as I had other plans. I wanted to go to the cinema and tenpin bowling with Rolly and some school friends. Suddenly the idea of spending my weekends with my father seemed uncool. The look on his face when I delivered this news would go on to haunt me in later years, although I barely registered it at the time. He was visibly crestfallen and withdrew into himself, confirming his acceptance of my new plans with grunts and nods. My mother too was clearly disappointed with me. Rather than making me feel guilty, if anything, I remember feeling rather pleased with myself at their reactions. I had reached an age where my parents' disapproval was a sought-after affirmation that told me I was making the right choice. I was just beginning to explore the notion of independence and a life outside the family home.

I remember nothing whatsoever of my afternoon with Rolly et al. I couldn't tell you what film we saw or if we even went bowling, let alone any of the finer details. In fact, other than Rolly, I couldn't even tell you who the other friends were. But I remember with complete clarity the scene as my father arrived home on the Sunday evening, carrying a giant faux-gold winner's trophy. In my younger years, my father would regularly take home a trophy or two from our weekend adventures. He had a shelf in his workshop crammed with gold, silver and bronze awards, each one holding a shared memory for the two of us that made them valuable far beyond their rendered plastic form. But this hadn't been the case for a long while now. I couldn't remember the last time I'd seen him win a race but it must have been at least four years earlier. He looked exhausted as he climbed the steps to greet us. Upon seeing him, my mother punched the air triumphantly and threw her arms around him as I stood back, looking sheepish. He smiled at me and handed me the trophy.

'That's for you, my boy.'

That was the end of my father's rallycross career. A career that could have been professional had he not decided to play it safe and obtain a more reliable and steady income following the birth of his son. A career that found new life at an amateur level when his young son showed an interest. A father and son team that travelled the south-west of England together, until the son drifted away from it. A victory that signalled the end of something significant. A change between us that could not be undone. My father and I drifted apart over the next few years. When I reached my twenties, we would reconnect and our relationship would go on to become even closer than in those early years. But this event seems – retrospectively – to mark the beginning of a period of time, lasting throughout my teens, where the two of us were lost to each other. To a lesser extent the same can be said of my relationship with my mother. The difference, I think, was her ability to see the selfish and unthinking actions of a troublesome teenager for what they were: a confused and destructive rebellion that would – thankfully – be temporary.

But even during those few years of relative estrangement, I kept the trophy my father had given me that day in pride of place on my windowsill. As if the pride I felt in him when I looked at it would sustain our relationship until the day came when we were able to find each other again.

■

The harsh laser-green glow of the cash machine screams into the darkness of the night. A woman with a bleached-blonde mass of tangled hair staggers and vomits against the beige brick wall to its left as her friends stand and watch. They pass around a cigarette that burns bright orange between their blood-red lips as their friend wipes her face with the back of her manicured hand. The vomit mixes with smeared black mascara and warm sour tears as she attempts to stand upright. Her tiny black dress rides up to reveal garish pink leopard print underwear. Two thick-necked young men drunkenly clamber past and shout obscenities at the woman as her friends roll their false-lashed eyes. One of the men mimes a sexual act with his sovereign-laden fingers as his designer-clad companion roars with intoxicated mirth. I try to feel hatred but cannot. As the night draws on, countless revellers spew their abuse and stomach contents into this illuminated space. As the sky turns a cavernous alien blue, a misshapen bearded man with dirt-blackened skin lays his blankets to the right of the machine and sits motionless beside his white Staffordshire bull terrier, whose sorrowful eyes sag under the weight of this life.

In the pale grey of morning, the hordes of identikit suits and briefcases arrive. They pass by unseeing as the misshapen bearded man tenderly wraps a blanket around his snoring companion. A businesswoman or man talking into a mobile phone approaches the cash machine, glances at the vomit, then at the bearded man and changes course. Time is passing, I think to myself. The night and the day, the dark and the light. These are things to take solace in, surely?

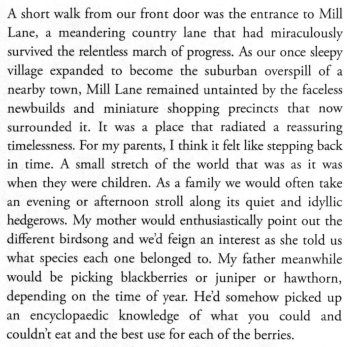

A short walk from our front door was the entrance to Mill Lane, a meandering country lane that had miraculously survived the relentless march of progress. As our once sleepy village expanded to become the suburban overspill of a nearby town, Mill Lane remained untainted by the faceless newbuilds and miniature shopping precincts that now surrounded it. It was a place that radiated a reassuring timelessness. For my parents, I think it felt like stepping back in time. A small stretch of the world that was as it was when they were children. As a family we would often take an evening or afternoon stroll along its quiet and idyllic hedgerows. My mother would enthusiastically point out the different birdsong and we'd feign an interest as she told us what species each one belonged to. My father meanwhile would be picking blackberries or juniper or hawthorn, depending on the time of year. He'd somehow picked up an encyclopaedic knowledge of what you could and couldn't eat and the best use for each of the berries.

In our teens, Jen and I would often walk the lane together in the dying embers of daylight. For us it was a place that offered a brief escape. A chance to smoke a clandestine cigarette or joint and gossip about our respective friends and life in general. By the time I was sixteen, I had a close and caring relationship with my sister. We would squabble from time to time, like all siblings, but for the most part we were allies and confidants. On one cold winter evening, we were strolling down the dark and deserted lane sharing a bottle of beer and debating who was the better band: Carter the Unstoppable Sex Machine or Ned's Atomic Dustbin. It was bonfire night and the sky rang out with distant whizzes and bangs and occasional flashes of light. Our breath rose in clouds of steam as we spoke. Jen had her wild curly mass of black hair tied back and, as she sipped on the beer, she looked far older than her years. She was rattling off Ned's lyrics as though quoting Shakespeare, gesticulating wildly as she did so ... but I wasn't really listening. I had something I needed to tell her.

I don't know exactly at what point in my life I had been certain that I was gay. Perhaps as soon as any notion of sex or sexuality had reared its wearisome head. But it was only in my mid-teens that I fully acknowledged it to myself. I had had no real intention of telling anyone. I figured it could wait until I met someone maybe. Then one night a few months earlier I got drunk with Rolly and blurted it out. At first he'd thought I was joking. Then, once he'd accepted that I was serious, he asked me if I fancied him. Many years later when we were in our late twenties, he would confess to me that he still felt ashamed that he'd said this in response to the news. But he was a sixteen-year-old boy and, in truth, I thought he reacted pretty well. I'd assured him I didn't fancy him and after a few minutes of uncomfortable silence he smiled at me and said, 'Fair enough, mate. Are you gonna hog all that beer or what then?'

Having told Rolly I knew that I had to tell Jen as soon as possible. She would already be upset at not being the first person I'd confided in and the longer I left it, the worse that would be. As with Rolly, deep down I knew that my sister would take the revelation in her stride and that it would have no negative impact on our relationship. That didn't make me any less nervous though. I abruptly stopped walking. She went on a few steps before realising I'd come to a halt. We then faced each other for the briefest moment as our breath rose then hung motionless in the air between us.

'So, I'm gay.'

She broke into a broad smile and narrowed her eyes. 'Well, duh. No shit, Sherlock.'

We embraced in the deserted country lane as rockets exploded in the sky above us, filling the air with neon glowing greens and reds. On reflection I should have guessed that Jen would have already known. Throughout our lives it always seemed that she knew me better than I knew myself. I'm not sure the same can be said the other way around though. I've always inherently understood my sister, but that's not quite the same thing. She has a capacity for empathy that is lacking in me. A selfless ability to not only understand what others may be going through but also to administer the care and advice required to help them. As we finished our beer and headed for home, I was so gladdened by her reaction to my news that I even told her I accepted her argument and that Ned's were indeed a better band than Carter. Which was, of course, a lie.

■

I search the woman's face for signs of anything beyond the silent rage. But there is nothing. Only anger. She slams the car door and skulks the crowded pavement with the assuredness of the well-rehearsed. The aching muscle memory of a mundane commute from one empty place to another. A lonely march into battle that will repeat each day until – finally – she is no longer capable or required. She is older than her years. Her unwashed grey hair frames a scowling, bespectacled smudge of wrinkles and creases. The hunch developing atop her bony, slender, tension-filled frame is the product of a life spent in the shadows. Shrinking and shrugging and squirming to avoid the light. She is surrounded by life but doesn't see it as it does not see her. Faces surround her. A thousand journeys, a thousand stories. My own among them. The young and old, the furious and fatigued, the loved and the lost. She sees none of them. She is alone with her sullenness. Is it regret? Was she once whole? Fulfilled? Hopeful? Or has it always been this way? A world with one inhabitant. The hateful slog of a life devoid of tenderness. I feel a flicker of something. A crack. For one fleeting second, I think I see myself. Not in her but somewhere in the thousand journeys, the thousand stories, that surround her.

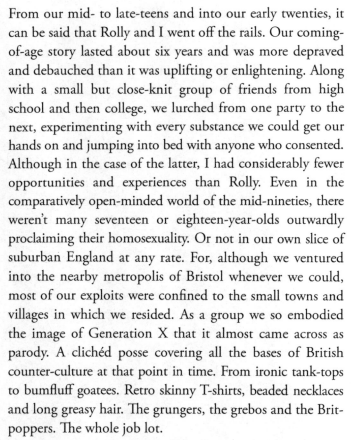

From our mid- to late-teens and into our early twenties, it can be said that Rolly and I went off the rails. Our coming-of-age story lasted about six years and was more depraved and debauched than it was uplifting or enlightening. Along with a small but close-knit group of friends from high school and then college, we lurched from one party to the next, experimenting with every substance we could get our hands on and jumping into bed with anyone who consented. Although in the case of the latter, I had considerably fewer opportunities and experiences than Rolly. Even in the comparatively open-minded world of the mid-nineties, there weren't many seventeen or eighteen-year-olds outwardly proclaiming their homosexuality. Or not in our own slice of suburban England at any rate. For, although we ventured into the nearby metropolis of Bristol whenever we could, most of our exploits were confined to the small towns and villages in which we resided. As a group we so embodied the image of Generation X that it almost came across as parody. A clichéd posse covering all the bases of British counter-culture at that point in time. From ironic tank-tops to bumfluff goatees. Retro skinny T-shirts, beaded necklaces and long greasy hair. The grungers, the grebos and the Brit-poppers. The whole job lot.

On one occasion, when I had just turned seventeen, Rolly – at that point sporting a Brett Anderson hairdo and a pair of purple corduroy flared trousers two sizes too small for him – excitedly advised us that he'd heard about a field party taking place outside a neighbouring town. Only one among our number could drive and so we all piled into an old beaten-up red Ford Fiesta. I remember it vividly: the front of the bonnet had rusted through and was held together with black masking tape. It had only one wing mirror and reeked of spoilt milk. There was no stereo so a small ghetto blaster with twin tape decks sat on the dashboard. Suede and These Animal Men crackled from the tinny speakers as we passed around joints and supermarket own-brand cans of lager.

We followed the directions Rolly had scribbled down as they led us down pitch-black muddy tracks. The car struggled onward, lurching into the darkness, straining under the weight of five or six expectant and stoned teenagers. In a woodland clearing, we found some fifty or so other cars abandoned haphazardly. We clambered from the Fiesta and wandered clumsily towards the sounds of electronic music and intoxicated revelry. The party was in full swing when we finally emerged from the darkness and into the light. Small bonfires were spread sporadically across the vista, each with its own group of illuminated bodies encircling it. A large sound system spewed out pulsating trance music that seemed to increase in speed and intensity, as well as volume, the closer we got to it.

We wandered aimlessly for a good while, inhaling the smoke-laden air and liberated ambience. Perhaps the intervening years have embellished my memories but looking back it seemed as though there were many hundreds there that night. An impromptu festival that encapsulated the freedom and spirit of that time in our lives. As we wandered, we passed endless streams of kindred souls with eyes dilated and radiant gurning smiles. Eventually we spotted some people we knew sitting around a campfire and decided to join them.

At some point an hour or so later, a friend of ours named Suzy introduced us to a giant grizzly bear of a man named, apparently, Slug. Slug was as wide as he was tall and he obscured the light of the fire when he sat down beside us. He wore a beanie hat that I could have comfortably climbed into, and a long green army jacket. His huge toothy grin was sly and knowing and I suddenly felt as though I had a decent understanding of what it felt like to be plankton.

'Hello my friends, would you like to see the light this evening?' he boomed in a deep growly voice. We all looked at each other nervously and then at Suzy.

'Slug gets the best acid going, you guys. Seriously, I wouldn't buy off anyone else.'

At this point in our fledging careers as dropouts, we'd mainly stuck to soap bar and cheap weed, although we'd recently started scoring low-quality speed – cut with lord knows what – from a friend of a friend in Bristol. In the months and years that followed, we'd go on to discover the triumph and the tragedy of ecstasy as well as the dirty purity of cocaine. But for now, we were – when all is said and done – still children. Infinitely less experienced than we considered ourselves to be and utterly ill equipped to drop acid. Thankfully all but one of us recognised this and started to decline the slightly creepy Slug's offer.

'Cool. I'll have some, mate,' cut in Rolly. I turned sharply to face him. He flashed me a cheeky grin and said, 'Come on, mate, let's do it.'

And that was that. I wasn't going to let Rolly take one on his own after all. Slug smiled menacingly and presented us with two tiny clear crystals.

'Microdots. The good shit, my beautiful children.'

We tentatively placed the minuscule dots on our tongues as instructed, while the others stared at us with a mixture of awe and incredulity.

'Best decision you'll ever make, my friends. See you on the other side.'

And with that, Slug was gone. He walked away from the light of the fire and disappeared into the darkness beyond.

What happened over the next six hours or so is largely unknown to me. Although, based on what I do remember, I consider this to be something of a blessing. My sense of first time and then reality as a whole began to warp and lose meaning as the tiny microdot set about poisoning my fragile young mind. Only the briefest flashes of memory remain. Someone asking me what it felt like. A dread-locked boy putting a caring arm around me and guiding me to a fireside. Stumbling and falling. A finger prodding me through the darkness as a distant voice murmured, 'Look at him, he's absolutely fucked.'

Bright, blurry lights and the endless looping rhythm of the music.

When I eventually began to regain some sense of self, I was standing in the corner of the field, facing a hedge. I was shivering with cold and dribbling great strands of stringy saliva. I turned around to see that the party had long since ended. The music had stopped and I was now standing in relative darkness. All that remained was a dozen or so tents, spread out across the field. I fuzzily and shakily wandered towards them. Something inside my still broken brain was yelling at me: 'Find Rolly.' I began to call his name as I stumbled around in the darkness among the beer cans and piles of ash. After a few minutes, a head emerged from one of the tents.

'Get in here, you dipshit.'

My friends, minus Rolly, were all crowded together inside a hastily-erected canvas. They cheered half-heartedly as I climbed in still shivering.

'Thought you weren't gonna make it for a while there, dude.'

They filled me in on the events of the night. Most of which I'd apparently spent staring, dribbling and falling over.

'Where's Rolly?'

'He went home with Suzy. He was in a right mess and she felt guilty for introducing you idiots to that Slug twat.'

'Is he alright?'

'Dunno. He spent the whole night clutching his crotch and saying he was desperate to take a piss but couldn't go. He was crying at one point.'

'Shit.'

I had no way of contacting my friend in those days, before the mobile phone was in widespread use, and so instead was forced to wait for many more hours, until our designated driver deemed himself fit and able. I sat hunched in the cold, wet tent, squashed and silent among my wasted comrades. Shivering and sweating as I fought off the fading waves of hallucinations that flitted and danced across the torchlit canvas and Cheshire Cat grinning faces.

The worry that I felt for my friend during those longest of hours is a memory that has stayed with me always. A level of unease I had hitherto not experienced. The chemicals still bleeding through my young mind and body cruelly intensifying my anxiety until the weight of it almost crushed me. I realised all at once not only how much I cared for and needed my friend, but also the extent to which I understood him. Through all his bravado and outward confidence, I knew inherently that he was not emotionally equipped to deal with the experience of the last six hours.

My relationships with those closest to me have always shared one common characteristic: the other party has always been the parental figure. The stronger half of the partnership that has, in varying ways, taken on the role of carer. My parents, grandfather and sister are all examples of this dynamic. It would also go on to be the case with the love of my life. But that night I understood for the first time that the reverse was true for Rolly and I. At this point in our lives at any rate. We would lie for each other and protect each other in equal measure but ultimately there was a vulnerability in him that only I could see. He was my responsibility. And in that sense, I had failed him that night. He was somewhere unknown to me. Alone and suffering. Beyond my reach.

As it turned out, Rolly was fine. He'd fallen asleep when he got back to Suzy's parents' house and had not woken up until that afternoon. Although he had indeed spent much of the night believing that he was desperate to urinate and could not do so. Despite the recklessness of the years that followed, neither of us ever touched that particular poison again.

✕

Notes from initial patient meeting: Wednesday 17th September

Upon arrival the patient shows clear signs that he is aware of my presence despite an outward appearance of catatonia. As the medical doctor's notes will attest, beyond his injuries he's in relatively good shape physically. A little malnourished perhaps. Would concur with initial speculation regards homelessness, i.e. doubtful unless very recent. Ran through standard questions around name, family, current whereabouts etc. Patient remained silent and without expression throughout.

However, when questioning about the attack itself, small but definite changes in facial expression evident. Of particular note: he looked at me when I mentioned the dog. The briefest of seconds but this is, in my opinion, the way through.

Certainly, enough evidence from this brief encounter to say with measured confidence that his silence/unresponsiveness is controlled and intentional. He's not incapable of speech/communication medically and, in my opinion, there's nothing to suggest any deep-rooted psychosomatic issue in this regard either.

Suggest one further session if missing persons continue to draw a blank.

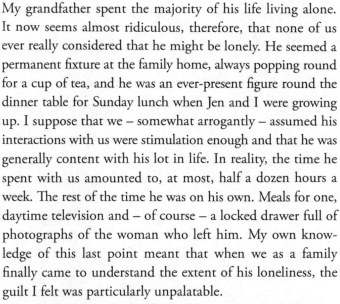

My grandfather spent the majority of his life living alone. It now seems almost ridiculous, therefore, that none of us ever really considered that he might be lonely. He seemed a permanent fixture at the family home, always popping round for a cup of tea, and he was an ever-present figure round the dinner table for Sunday lunch when Jen and I were growing up. I suppose that we – somewhat arrogantly – assumed his interactions with us were stimulation enough and that he was generally content with his lot in life. In reality, the time he spent with us amounted to, at most, half a dozen hours a week. The rest of the time he was on his own. Meals for one, daytime television and – of course – a locked drawer full of photographs of the woman who left him. My own know-ledge of this last point meant that when we as a family finally came to understand the extent of his loneliness, the guilt I felt was particularly unpalatable.

I was sitting at the kitchen table one morning slurping down a bowl of sugary cereal as Jen and my mother argued somewhere behind me. I can't remember what they were arguing about as, in truth, it was a daily occurrence by this point. Jen had reached an age where everything my mother said seemed to infuriate her. Likewise, my mother seemed suddenly incapable of reacting to whatever Jen uttered with anything other than stern disapproval. I'd long since learnt to block out their bickering and was absentmindedly listen-ing to the radio as it chattered away in the background. It was set to a local station and they were discussing the launch of a new care in the community programme. This included a phone-in about the realities of day-to-day life as an elderly or vulnerable member of society.

It took a few seconds for my brain to register the sound of my grandfather's voice. Then a few seconds more to accept that I wasn't simply imagining it.

'Oi, listen! That's Grandpa.'

Jen and my mother both turned to face me mid-argument, scowls still plastered across their faces. Then they too registered exactly what they were hearing. Without a word, they both sat down beside me at the table and we listened as our loved one poured out his heart to a total stranger.

'I wake up and the first thing I think is, "Oh no, another bloody day." I'm just so lonely.'

Jen and I pulled something like a grimace at this, while my mother's face was less easy to read.

'The days are just empty, you know? I have nothing to do … nowhere to be.'

'And what about your family, caller? Isn't there anyone that could make some time for you … to be with you?'

'There's my daughter and her family. They're very good to me and I'm lucky to have them. But they've got lives of their own, you know? I can't expect them to find the time for a silly old fool like me.'

We all sat in silence for what felt like an age. The breakfast show host was at least halfway through the next call before my mother spoke.

'How dare he do that. How dare he do that to us.'

With hindsight it's now obvious that my mother was in a state of shock and denial. She doted on her father just as she doted on Jen and me. The pain of what she'd just heard was too much to process right away. At that moment, however, her apparent fury only added to the utter disbelief that my sister and I were experiencing. Jen in particular visibly recoiled at my mother's words.

'For Christ's sake, Mum. He's upset, how can you be angry?'

My mother stormed from the room. She must've called my father at work because within an hour he had arrived home. By that time, she was weeping uncontrollably and Jen and I were trying in vain to console her. My father took her in his arms, gently rocking and shushing her like a child. His tenderness towards her at that moment was such that it would go on, in part, to shape my own idea of what a loving partnership should look like. Not a hint of hesitation or awkwardness. He knew instinctively what she needed from him and he gave it, unreservedly. She quietened in his arms, her sobs becoming first whimpers and then no more than uneven intakes of breath.

My father didn't go back to work that day. In fact, nobody went to work or college. Instead, we talked for hours about my grandfather. In doing so, we uncovered many difficult truths. For instance, we realised that, while he would regularly drop by for a cuppa and a chat, we almost never went to visit him at his house anymore. We also acknowledged that, because we as a family no longer sat down to a Sunday lunch every week, come what may, it meant that his once regular invite was now increasingly sporadic and infrequent. In doing this we inevitably exposed the growing cracks in our own relationships with one another. As Jen and I got older, the time we spent as a foursome was diminishing at a relentless pace. We didn't specifically voice this to each other, but the subtext was clear enough.

My mother remained totally distraught throughout. She pored over every conversation she'd had with her father over the last few months and years. Chastising herself for the fact that every time they'd spoken it had always been about her – the problems and stresses in her world – but never about him: how *he* was doing or what was going on in *his* life. We were all guilty of this though. He had always been such a kind, gentle and smiling presence in our lives. A straight-forward constant whose beauty lay in his reliability and apparent simplicity. He was always there for us with a consoling word or selfless gesture. *For* us rather than *with* us.

We strategized throughout the afternoon. A family of four waking up to the reality that we'd forgotten that we were actually a family of five. We vowed that Grandpa would always be invited for Sunday lunch, no matter how many of us were there. We created a new ritual of Monday night fish 'n' chips round Grandpa's house. Again, even if only one of us could make it, we promised each other that he would never eat alone on a Monday evening again. My father committed to spending a few hours a week with him working on his garden and Jen and I both agreed to phone him at least once a week each from here on in.

We decided not to tell him that we'd heard the radio interview. Although, looking back, he probably guessed we had done as we all turned up unannounced on his doorstep that evening laden with bags of chips and stinking of vinegar. My mother must have hugged him a hundred times during the few hours that we were there. My father dropped hints about his garden needing a bit of work as Jen earnestly enquired as to how he was feeling. Subtle we were not. But our enthusiasm was genuine and I think this was evident as he seemed to radiate an uncomplicated happiness through-out. We basked in the warmth of his company. I remember looking at him that evening as he laughed heartily from behind his bushy moustache and thinking how blessed I was to have him in my life.

For the record, we kept our promises. From that moment on, I don't think a single day went by without my mother either dropping in on her father or inviting him over. Likewise, he gained a full-time gardener in the shape of my father. My grandfather had always treated me like the golden child. He put me on a pedestal from a young age and I'd always known that his love for me – like that of my mother and father – was unconditional. I hope then, for my part, that from that day onward I was able to convey through my actions that the feeling was mutual.

■

A large black beak jabs rhythmically at the scant darkened flesh hanging from the splayed and shattered remains. A decaying unidentifiable lump that once, not so long ago, breathed and soared with life. Now a smear on the asphalt. The raven looks up as a distant mechanical rumble pierces the silence. It watches with a curious cocked head as a mass of blinding light and metal screams through the night towards it. An unfathomable monster reflected in the pitch-black pools of the raven's eye. A message reaches the brain a heartbeat before contact and the bird lurches to the safety of the roadside. The monster does not swerve or deviate. Its cold, dead frame brushes the flailing wing of the raven as it shrieks past. The bird cocks its head the other way as it observes the monster disappear into the night amid an alien red glow. It bounces back to the broken smear of bone and drying flesh. Where once blood pulsed, the black beak jabs in time with its own pounding heart. It feasts uncomprehendingly in the damp quiet of the night, as an endless army of cold, dead monsters with blinding lights and metallic roars scream through the darkness.

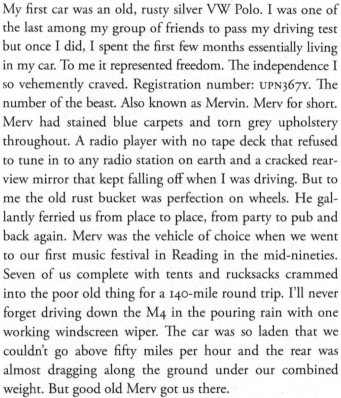

My first car was an old, rusty silver VW Polo. I was one of the last among my group of friends to pass my driving test but once I did, I spent the first few months essentially living in my car. To me it represented freedom. The independence I so vehemently craved. Registration number: UPN367Y. The number of the beast. Also known as Mervin. Merv for short. Merv had stained blue carpets and torn grey upholstery throughout. A radio player with no tape deck that refused to tune in to any radio station on earth and a cracked rear-view mirror that kept falling off when I was driving. But to me the old rust bucket was perfection on wheels. He gallantly ferried us from place to place, from party to pub and back again. Merv was the vehicle of choice when we went to our first music festival in Reading in the mid-nineties. Seven of us complete with tents and rucksacks crammed into the poor old thing for a 140-mile round trip. I'll never forget driving down the M4 in the pouring rain with one working windscreen wiper. The car was so laden that we couldn't go above fifty miles per hour and the rear was almost dragging along the ground under our combined weight. But good old Merv got us there.

I remember one occasion when I spent the evening at my friend Tony's house. His folks were away for the night and he lived out in the sticks, so I picked up Rolly en route and drove Merv out into deepest darkest Somerset. We spent the evening getting stoned and playing Mario Kart. In the early hours of the morning I decided – in that way that only a reckless and slightly moronic teenager can do – that I was perfectly fit to drive home. Rolly had all but passed out and announced that he intended to stay the night at Tony's. Which of course is what I should have done. But in my infinite wisdom, I was determined that Merv and I should head off into the night.

I was so stoned that I drove along the pitch-black country lanes at what must have been about fifteen miles per hour. A paranoid red-eyed mess startled by every noise or movement. Then, after about twenty minutes, I zoned out and drove Merv off the road and into a ditch. I sat there stunned for a few minutes, not quite believing what had happened. My heart was racing and I was in danger of descending into blind panic. Merv was sat tilted at a forty-five degree angle. The engine had stalled upon impact but it started without complaint when I turned the key. Not that it mattered of course. There was no way Merv was budging. My panic finally subsided to be replaced by a brief and inexplicable fit of the giggles. Eventually I retained some degree of composure and began to contemplate my next move.

Having spotted a road sign, I wandered down the lane towards the nearest village. Thankfully this proved to be only half a mile or so away and awaiting me upon arrival was the glorious sight of a phone box. Tony had a car but, in truth, it never even crossed my mind to call him. Without any hesitation or fear of consequence, I phoned my father. After ringing for what felt like minutes, it was thankfully he who picked up. I say thankfully as, if my mother had picked up, she would have instantly been so riddled with worry and panic at the idea that I'd been in a car accident that within seconds every emergency service vehicle available across the county would doubtless have been speeding through the night to reach me with sirens howling. I was sobering up by now but I'm sure I still sounded in a state as I hastily blurted out my explanation of events to him, naturally omitting the fact that I had been immeasurably stoned when I drove the car very slowly into a ditch. He remained silent throughout until eventually I told him the name of the village I was in and asked him to come and get me.

'I'm on my way.'

It took my father about forty minutes to reach me, during which time I'd all but sobered up. He placed his hand on my shoulder and looked me up and down.

'You okay?'

'Yes. A bit shaken. But … Dad … the car.'

'Show me.'

We drove through the darkness to where Merv lay abandoned.

'You should have put the hazard lights on.'

That was as close as he got to reprimanding me that night. Even though it must have been obvious that, at the very least, I'd been inconceivably careless. Even though it was 3:30 in the morning and I'd woken him up. Even though we'd barely spoken to each other in the last few months. I stood to one side as he tied a rope from his tow bar to Merv's front bumper and very slowly pulled the sorry old car from the ditch. He wouldn't let me drive myself home but instead shortened the rope that bound the two vehicles and told me to sit in my car and steer as he towed me home.

Perhaps it was the weed still leaving my system, but I couldn't fail to see the symbolism of the journey home that followed thereafter. My father had rescued me and was now leading me to safety. To home. Through the darkness and into the dawning light of a new day. Just as he always had done and always would do, for the rest of his life. I sat in silence watching the back of his head through the rear window of the vehicle in front, with the twisting, turning road beyond. My guide, showing me the way once again. Picking me up when I fall and carrying me home when I'm too weak to manage it under my own steam. He never told my mother that he'd had to pull the car from the ditch. He told her it had simply broken down and that he would fix it. Nothing to worry about.

Incidentally, Merv lived to fight another day. He eventually conked out for good about eighteen months later. But I kept the number plate, UPN367Y, as a memento. It still hangs above the doorframe of my spare bedroom.

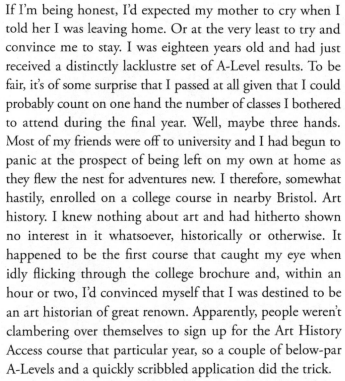

If I'm being honest, I'd expected my mother to cry when I told her I was leaving home. Or at the very least to try and convince me to stay. I was eighteen years old and had just received a distinctly lacklustre set of A-Level results. To be fair, it's of some surprise that I passed at all given that I could probably count on one hand the number of classes I bothered to attend during the final year. Well, maybe three hands. Most of my friends were off to university and I had begun to panic at the prospect of being left on my own at home as they flew the nest for adventures new. I therefore, somewhat hastily, enrolled on a college course in nearby Bristol. Art history. I knew nothing about art and had hitherto shown no interest in it whatsoever, historically or otherwise. It happened to be the first course that caught my eye when idly flicking through the college brochure and, within an hour or two, I'd convinced myself that I was destined to be an art historian of great renown. Apparently, people weren't clambering over themselves to sign up for the Art History Access course that particular year, so a couple of below-par A-Levels and a quickly scribbled application did the trick.

A friend of a friend of a friend had a cheap room going in a shared house near the city centre and I leapt at the chance. In just a few days I'd transformed myself from stay-at-home failure to young art historian off to the bright lights of the big city. I was naturally feeling pretty pleased with myself as I arrived home to tell my family the big news. My father reacted to type by launching into a barrage of financially themed questions. How would I afford this, exactly? Was I expecting him to pay for it? Did I have a job lined up? Jen also reacted as expected by immediately planning her first stay over in the big city. Her wide-eyed excitement at the news added to my completely unwarranted sense of achievement. My mother, however, didn't react at all as I'd anticipated. No tears or hysteria. No desperate declarations that the family couldn't cope without the angelic firstborn.

Instead, she met the news with a quiet resignation. She offered up a strange and somewhat distant smile, the like of which I'd not seen on her before. She even interrupted my father's objections mid-rant. 'Now, now. I'm sure we can work something out if this is what you want, my love.'

Her eyes seemed slightly glazed over, almost as if unseeing. For this reason, I quickly convinced myself that the enormity of my news simply hadn't hit home yet. The tears and general devastation were pending. Nevertheless, I recall feeling a touch miffed at not being given the overdramatic scene for which I'd prepped myself. Over the next few days, I would regularly attempt to gently coax the desired histrionics from her. I'd begin sentences with phrases like, 'When I'm gone,' or, 'Once it's just the three of you.' But to my continued chagrin, none of this subtle cajoling seemed to come remotely close to opening the floodgates. She remained dry-cheeked and pragmatic throughout.

Then one evening, about a week before I was due to leave for Bristol, I arrived home to hear the muffled but unmistakable sounds of sobbing coming from somewhere in the house. I followed the sounds up the stairs and towards my parents' bedroom. I steeled myself for the emotional outpouring I was about to receive. I'd been expecting this after all. Behind the door at which I now stood, doubtless sat my weeping mother surrounded by photo albums charting my journey from babe-in-arms to dashing independent young man and aspiring art historian. I gingerly knocked on the door.

To my surprise, it was my father's voice I heard next. 'Come in, come in.'

As I tentatively swung open the door, the scene before me was not entirely as I had foreseen. There were no photographs strewn about the place for a start. My mother and father were kneeling on the floor in an embrace. My mother was indeed weeping but as they both turned to face me, huge grins were stretched across both their faces. As my father spoke, his voice cracked with something that resembled – but wasn't quite – nervous laughter.

'Go fetch your sister. We need to tell you both something.'

A few weeks before I'd delivered my 'big news', my mother had found a small lump in her breast while showering. Following a scan, her doctor had advised her that she needed a biopsy. The biopsy revealed that the lump was cancerous. She had received that news an hour or so before my grand announcement. A surgeon had then removed a small amount of tissue from around the lump to determine if the cancer was spreading. It wasn't. But they still needed to remove the lump immediately and so – earlier that day – she had had a lumpectomy. Only when they got home less than an hour before I had, did my mother allow herself to accept that the ordeal was over.

She had shouldered the weight of all of this herself, only telling my father once she'd had it confirmed that the cancer hadn't spread, then convincing him to keep it from Jen and me until the operation was complete. I had wanted my mother to worry about me. To beg me to stay at home. To be heartbroken at my news. I had even attempted to stimulate such emotions in her in the days that followed my proclamation. All the while, my mother had been forced to face her own mortality and chosen to do so alone. Her love for her family and desire to protect us from harm and pain had led her to spare us the burden of fear and anxiety. To shield us from the potential devastation for as long as she was able. Even in the face of death, she had put our emotional needs before her own.

Jen and I both broke down and wept upon hearing the news. At this, our mother gathered us in her arms. She comforted and quietened us. The lioness protecting her pride, teeth bared in the face of any threat to her vulnerable cubs.

During the next week, we all naturally doted on her. Breakfast in bed, endless cups of tea and a limitless supply of foot massages from my father. My grandfather, upon hearing the news, arrived bearing huge bags of pink and white marshmallows.

On the evening before I left for Bristol, she came into my bedroom and sat beside me on the bed. 'You know your father and I are proud of you, don't you?'

I didn't know how to react to this. I wanted to tell her that they shouldn't be. That I was selfish and irresponsible and didn't want to study stupid art history. I wanted to tell her that I'd all but failed my A-Levels and rather than facing up to it, I was running away. And that if I ever lost her, I would be nothing. A shadow. I wanted to tell her that she was my soul. That my heart beat for her. But I said none of this.

'Yeah, of course, Mum. And don't worry, I'll be fine. It's only up the road.'

'I'm not worried, my love. You're my soldier. The world won't know what's hit it.'

■

The woman in front of me writhes beneath her stained and ill-fitted garments. She mutters and spits. Steam rises from her twitching mouth into the cold night as she spews quiet profanities at unseen protagonists long gone or never there. She is on the cusp of losing control of something. All jerking limbs and racing thoughts. She is a many-splintered thing. The milk-skinned boy behind me looks doggedly at the pavement beneath his foraged footwear. As if he cannot stand to see his own future in the eyes of the lost and broken figures waiting on this frozen spot. The black river below reflects the garish glow of the city above it. The rich odour of stewing flesh and vegetables permeates the air. Down the line, the sustenance given by kindly souls offers respite and the strength required to turn another page. To read on. This tired narrative of luckless castaways. The outtakes of an empty epic that endlessly lurches from one crisis to the next. Scene. End scene.

Shuffle. Stand. Shuffle. Stand. I hold out my shaking dirt-smeared hands and look away from the pitying features of a better man than I. I? When was I last I? The polystyrene cup slowly burns my hands as I leave that place. The empty cavernous space is unquiet for the first time in … in? An acknowledgement. I'm not fit to stand among those forms. Those unmissed missing. I'm an imposter.

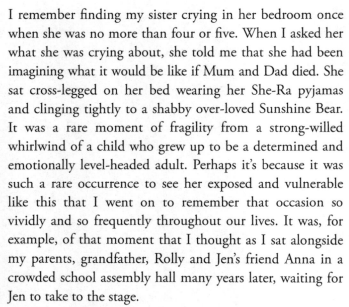

I remember finding my sister crying in her bedroom once when she was no more than four or five. When I asked her what she was crying about, she told me that she had been imagining what it would be like if Mum and Dad died. She sat cross-legged on her bed wearing her She-Ra pyjamas and clinging tightly to a shabby over-loved Sunshine Bear. It was a rare moment of fragility from a strong-willed whirlwind of a child who grew up to be a determined and emotionally level-headed adult. Perhaps it's because it was such a rare occurrence to see her exposed and vulnerable like this that I went on to remember that occasion so vividly and so frequently throughout our lives. It was, for example, of that moment that I thought as I sat alongside my parents, grandfather, Rolly and Jen's friend Anna in a crowded school assembly hall many years later, waiting for Jen to take to the stage.

Rolly and I had just finished our A-Levels and Jen and Anna their GCSEs. Jen was a grade A student in most subjects, but her passion had always been drama. She had dreams of RADA and, although that particular ambition would never be fulfilled, she would go on to be accepted into a very auspicious drama school in London a few years later. At the end of each school year, the drama departments of both Borechester High School for Girls and Boys would join forces to put on a play that would be open to the public. Usually this would result in a dozen or so of the participants' parents sitting along the front row of an otherwise empty assembly hall. I hadn't been for many years but my mother and father never missed a show. Over the years, they'd sat through largely underwhelming productions of everything from *King Lear* to *Joseph and the Amazing Technicolor Dreamcoat* in order to show their support for their beloved daughter. This one was to be different though.

At the end of the previous year, the girls' school had hired a new drama teacher. A young and ambitious woman named Ms Hickson. Or, as she insisted her class call her, Ms H. She had quickly become something of a local celebrity. An agreeably alternative, grungy-looking woman with some radical ideas. Well, radical by the standards of high school drama productions at any rate. Throughout the year, she'd taken the students into the nearby towns and villages to perform impromptu and often improvised street theatre. She'd also put on ambitious interpretations of *1984* and *Oedipus Rex*. She'd caused such a stir among parents that she'd recently been interviewed by the local newspaper following readers' letters of concern about her 'unique' teaching techniques and a spattering of accusations that she was pushing her 'feminist agenda' onto the girls. Perish the thought. For obvious reasons, she was nothing short of a hero to Jen and her classmates. It was during this newspaper interview that she announced that the end-of-term play this year would be *Hamlet*. With a twist, of course. The main modification being that Hamlet would be recast as female and Ophelia as male.

This bold-for-the-time-and-place reimagining was doubtless the reason behind the hundred-seater hall being full to bursting for the first time in living memory but, in truth, it wasn't why I was there. Jen had been cast as Hamlet. Her first leading role. We were thrilled for her but I was also increasingly nervous. As the crowd murmured in anticipation, I was imagining the chubby-faced child sat cross-legged on her bed hugging her grubby Care Bear to the point of suffocation. I felt an overwhelming desire to protect my baby sister at that moment. All nonsense of course. I was projecting my own fear of public speaking onto my self-assured and talented sibling. Jen was brilliant.

My parents clasped each other's hands with white-knuckle intensity as she took to the stage. Then swelled with pride and beamed with moist-eyed smiles as she held the assembly hall spellbound. My grandfather gave an impromptu one-man standing ovation at the end of act three, scene one as Jen cast aside her broad-shouldered Ophelia, a scene that reduced Anna, who sat beside me, to a sniffling mess. Alas, poor Rolly, caught up in the excitement of it all, insisted on booing every time Claudius – a small plump girl with spectacle lenses so thick her eyes looked as though they belonged on someone else's face – took to the stage.

I was mesmerised by my little sister as she commanded the room. I sat breathless as she conveyed the weight of moral struggle, the all-consuming guilt and sense of honour with an authenticity and passion way beyond her years. I'd always been proud of Jen but that afternoon I was in awe of her so completely that I forgot my cool veneer of teenage indifference as the tatty and moth-eaten curtain fell. I stood and whooped and cheered at the top of my voice. As she took her bow, she no longer bore a resemblance to the chubby little girl in the She-Ra pyjamas. For the first time I looked at her and saw a woman. Her black curls were slicked back to reveal the striking and defined features of a performer who would go on to command the stage of many a grander room than this. Her broad smile was not that of a girl overwhelmed but an assured actor gracefully accepting the plaudits she'd earned. There were many watery eyes in the room, but hers were not among them.

When we found her backstage, she was in conversation with Ms H. The older woman was gushing with praise for her young prodigy and, as we approached, she flung her arms theatrically aloft.

'Your daughter is a star! I was just telling her that this is just the beginning. Her talent can never fall short of her desire.'

My father looked a little embarrassed as my mother positively glowed with pride. Jen caught my gaze and rolled her eyes as Ms H continued to lavish acclaim on her, as though she wasn't standing beside her.

Rolly, Anna and my grandfather all joined us for pizza that evening. An occasion notable for a few things, not least of which for being an increasingly rare example of the whole family eating together. Most of all though, I remember Jen. As soon as we'd left the school, she was my little sister again. She gossiped with Anna, teased Rolly and momentarily copped a strop when my mother and father refused to let her have a glass of wine with her food. The transformation was both eerie and comforting. The clock had stopped. Time's relentless march had paused and, in that moment, we were as we'd always been. A family – outside of time. We smiled and laughed, we squabbled and huffed. It was as it had been but not as it would be. That afternoon we'd glimpsed the future and, for one of us at least, it was wonderful. A place full of possibility and excitement. But it could wait.

■

The creature prowls the dawn-lit detritus with a nervous-ness so apparent that it is almost audible in the cold stillness of this place. Its ribcage presses against a thin layer of mange-ridden red and yellow fur as though death is already in residence within. It paws through the discarded and disposable remnants of the city in search of anything that might stave off the burning hunger.

A light flickers into life behind a window countless storeys above the creature's head, beyond the wretched boundaries of its understanding. It looks up with a start and then freezes, remaining in this motionless state of alert-ness for some time. Then, as it turns, it sees me. As it holds my gaze, I can feel its fear. Its infected eyes are weeping and an ear has been ripped open. The torn flesh is crusted with dark, dried blood. It bares its yellow teeth but then imme-diately cowers, head down, eyes looking up, still staring into my own. It whimpers and whines, then turns and runs into the shadows and the infinite nothing beyond.

Deep in those eyes, I knew its sorrow. I felt it. I was feeling. Its lost helpless gaze burned through something. An innocent desperate need for help scorched onto a blank, lifeless canvas. Hope and pain flooding an empty space. A tear runs down my cheek and I lift my hand to feel it. Then I weep and sob and howl into the void.

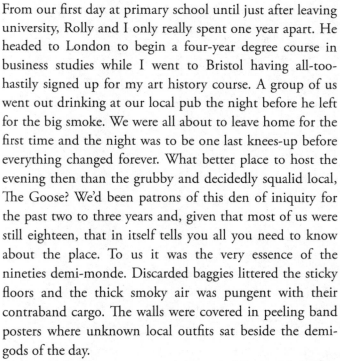

From our first day at primary school until just after leaving university, Rolly and I only really spent one year apart. He headed to London to begin a four-year degree course in business studies while I went to Bristol having all-too-hastily signed up for my art history course. A group of us went out drinking at our local pub the night before he left for the big smoke. We were all about to leave home for the first time and the night was to be one last knees-up before everything changed forever. What better place to host the evening then than the grubby and decidedly squalid local, The Goose? We'd been patrons of this den of iniquity for the past two to three years and, given that most of us were still eighteen, that in itself tells you all you need to know about the place. To us it was the very essence of the nineties demi-monde. Discarded baggies littered the sticky floors and the thick smoky air was pungent with their contraband cargo. The walls were covered in peeling band posters where unknown local outfits sat beside the demi-gods of the day.

It was the spot where most of us had got drunk for the first time and it held many a fond memory for each of us. It's where Tony lost his virginity to the hippy barmaid Nikki, who only afterwards found out his real age and hadn't spoken to any of us since. It's where our friend Gavin once spent the whole night locked in on his own, having passed out in the toilets and woken up to find himself alone. It was also the scene of my only sexual encounter with a girl.

A green-eyed, pink-haired, pierced-lipped punk who pounced on me in a dark corner of the beer garden one night. We kissed in a sloppy drunken revelry before she thrust her hand down my trousers to discover a limp and unstimulated set of genitalia. This pub represented something to us that none of us were capable of putting into words, but all instinctively understood. It was also starting to look dated by this point. Its once edgy alternative ambience now verged on the clichéd. This was the end of something. An era, our teenage dreams, the scene that shaped our identities. A few months after we all left, The Goose was shut down to later reopen as a wine bar named Charlie's. But tonight, for one last time, it was ours.

As nights at The Goose went, it was largely uneventful, although nobody minded. We sat huddled together under the flickering orange lights as some fuzzy forgotten indie music crackled from the speakers. We did something we'd not done before as a group: we reminisced, recalling the moments that had shaped our lives over the last few years and in doing so afforded them a new significance. Then, as I looked across at Rolly, the truth of our departure seemed to hit me all at once and I began to cry. I was incapable of verbalising my sadness and thankfully didn't try to. My friends put tender supporting arms around me and in the end most of us were sobbing weakly into our pints. Mercifully, this melancholy passed and, as the night lurched on, we drank ourselves into a stupor.

The following morning I met up with Rolly just before his parents drove him to London. From one life to another. We exchanged mixtapes that we'd made for one another, full of songs that for whatever reason remind us of each other. Long, sprawling, wallowing odes to sadness by The

Cure. Triumphant, anthemic floor-fillers by Pulp and Gene. Captured moments of our lives together. We embraced and soberly said our goodbyes, vowing to write and visit whenever possible. That walk back from Rolly's to mine seemed like the loneliest of my life up to that point. I sat in my room and packed my bags for Bristol, suffocating under the weight of a million conflicting emotions.

The following year was one of great significance to each of us for very different reasons. Rolly collapsed into London life seamlessly and met many of the people who would go on to become important parts of both our lives, including most significantly a girl named Tabitha, who he would go on to marry. We would write to each other regularly throughout the year and keep each other up to date on our new lives. We each visited the other once and of course made plenty of phone calls. But it was the letters that I remember being of most significance that year.

Although I would go on to very happily call Bristol my home in later years, that first experience of it was not a positive one for me. My new housemates were a few years older than me and a good deal more worldly. I attached myself to their social group and found that I was quickly drawn into a spinning, drowning world of ecstasy and cocaine. Of endless clawing, nightmarish raves where the walls of reality crumbled amid the warped blur of the night. A year of lonely excess followed wherein I lost myself utterly as the venoms pierced the psyche. I was always somehow removed from those around me. The bonds forged were paper thin. I was and remained an outsider. Accepted but never really known to anyone. Many lifelong anxieties and insecurities were forged during that year and there were many times when only Rolly's letters kept me sane. I'd open them hungrily and then sink into their nostalgia. In my letters back to him, I never really confided how miserable I'd become but the consoling nature of his writing suggested at least some level of understanding.

I passed my art history course, although looking back I get the impression it may have been harder not to. But I got the extra credit I needed from it and applied for a media studies degree in a lesser-known London university. Rolly and I were then reunited in the big smoke where we shared a house with three other layabouts and embarked on many happy adventures. That year in Bristol was, when all is said and done, no more than a minor setback. And yet, it was the first time in my life that I questioned the essence of myself. Without those I loved and who loved me, who was I, really?

✕

Notes from follow-up patient meeting: Friday 19th September

Patient is sitting up and has, in the last few hours, eaten of his own accord for the first time. I proceed once more with my attempt to ascertain his identity.

'Are you ready to talk about what happened to you?'

'Is there someone who'll be looking for you that we can get in touch with?'

'You must be as bored of all these questions as I am. How about helping me out here?'

'I'm sure you've looked better but I'm assured you'll make a full recovery ... so, that's great, isn't it?'

(Pause)

'What about the dog? Ah, yes ... hello there, that resonates, doesn't it? I'd like to talk to you about the dog, if that's okay? I thought you'd be worried about him so I paid him a visit.'

And then he spoke at last. A quiet, hoarse whisper, barely audible. I endeavoured to show little or no surprise and carried on as planned.

'Is ... is he okay?'

'Yes and no. He's recovering from the operation and the prognosis is positive. But he's clearly distressed. I'd expect he could do with seeing a face he recognises.'

'He's not used to people. He doesn't trust them.'

'What's his name?'

The patient smiles, then winces at the pain the action causes to his bruised and battered face.

'I call him Marmite.'

'Ha … yes, that works. Does he belong to you?'

'He … no. He helped me.'

'I see. I expect you'd like to see him?'

'Very much.'

The patient breathes in a deep sigh and then looks me squarely in the eye for the first time.

'What do I need to do to make that happen?'

≡

My grandfather was the last of my loved ones that I came out to. Well, that's not entirely true as I never actually told him, per se. I'd always reasoned that there was no need to, as anything so adult a topic as sexuality seemed so far outside the parameters of our relationship. I suppose, if I'm entirely honest, I was also a touch fearful of doing so. The generation gap perhaps meant that I was slightly less confident of getting the supportive and accepting response I'd received from my parents when I finally told them just before leaving for London.

During my time at university, we would speak once a week on the phone. We'd take turns to call each other at exactly 7:00 pm every Thursday night. A rigid and reliable constant amid the chaos of student life. An anchor that helped ensure the comfort and safety of home was never out of reach, even when the stormy waters threatened to engulf me.

I sat on the stairs waiting for his call one cold, damp evening. Although it was always cold and damp in that particular house. A tumbledown Victorian terrace with no central heating, nicotine-coated walls and stained threadbare carpets of garish purple and orange. Fixed to the wall at the bottom of the stairs was a pay phone the size and weight of a breezeblock. We had to insert 10p to make a call and for that reason I think I must've been the only one who actually used it the entire time we were there. It was five past seven. My grandfather was late. With anyone else this would of course be of no concern, but he was never late. Punctuality was one of a number of disciplines he'd successfully passed down to his eldest grandchild. It was therefore with something close to panic that I grabbed for the phone when it finally rang a few minutes later.

'Hi, Grandpa.'

A brief silence ensued before he answered.

'Your sister's just been telling me that you're a Homo sapiens?'

Grandpa would regularly mix up his words in this manner. I once received a letter from him asking me if I thought my parents would like an annual membership to the National Front as an anniversary gift. It took me most of the afternoon to realise that he'd meant the National Trust. His true meaning on this occasion, however, was clear.

'Oh … did she?'

I was going to kill her. How dare she take it upon herself to tell him without discussing it with me first.

'I'm a bit cross to be honest with you, my boy.'

My heart sank. 'Cross?'

'Why didn't you tell me yourself? That's what I'd like to know.'

I had no answer for this and sat dumbstruck as the phoneline crackled across the miles that separated us.

'You still there?'

'Yes … sorry.'

'Well?'

'Is it … is it a problem?'

'What?'

'That I'm gay.'

'Don't be so bloody stupid. You know me better than that. Which is exactly why I want to know why you haven't told me yourself.'

'I'm sorry, Grandpa. I wasn't sure you'd … I mean, I didn't want to…'

'Now you listen here. You're my grandson. I don't care if you're gay, straight or French. The point is you can tell me anything, okay?'

And I suddenly realised that I could. Of course I could. Unconditional love is exactly that. My grandfather had never given me any reason at all to think he'd harbour any of the ignorance and prejudice unfortunately not so uncommon among his demographic. In fact, barring a bizarre mistrust of the French, he'd always proved himself to be an accepting and unjudgmental man. I felt slightly ashamed of myself for doubting him. I apologised and the conversation soon veered off into more familiar waters. Our relationship thereafter was utterly unaffected. We were grandfather and grandson, as ageless and mutually proud of each other as we'd always been. Even though those relationship parameters I mentioned meant that we never really spoke of such matters again, I was always incredibly touched when, in the years that followed, I'd receive Christmas cards emblazoned with the message 'To my grandson and his partner.' Exactly where he managed to find such gender-neutral greetings cards in the early years of the twenty-first century remains a mystery to me.

As soon as I'd put down the phone to him that evening, it began to ring again.

'I'm sorry, I'm sorry. I didn't mean to let it slip!'

Jen was beside herself with worry and I found that I simply couldn't be angry with her. She was relieved to hear how the conversation had gone and reduced to a fit of giggles when I told her that our grandfather had asked me if I was a Homo sapiens.

■

I used to know this place. This city. I used to crave its vibrancy and bathe in its possibility. It once seemed a living, breathing thing to me. Almost a layer. It challenged and provoked. Nurtured and forgave. Perhaps that's why I came here again. If I was to be swallowed … drowned … lost, then it could only be under its neon blanket. Or maybe some bleeding scrap of subconscious believed it could weave its diverse tapestry across the empty space like a healing spider's web. In lostness that I might find some forgotten abandoned strand of myself and be born anew. Reformed and remoulded by some youthful spark hitherto assumed extinguished in the smouldering smoke of passing time.

But it is not a layer. There is no sanctuary here. No kindness in the unseen corners of this lifeless skeleton. No meaning in the shadows. It is inanimate. A vessel built to accommodate our headless, unceasing obliteration. A scar on the skin of the world. A symptom of the disease that spreads and sucks and drains. Beyond the bright lights there is a darkness so vast and so cold and it will swallow you whole.

And yet.

And yet I look now for the creature whose eyes were filled with a sorrow that reached into the void and found … something still beating. A tenderness. I search the spaces in-between. Under, behind, out of sight. I look through the cracks. Where are you? I will find you.

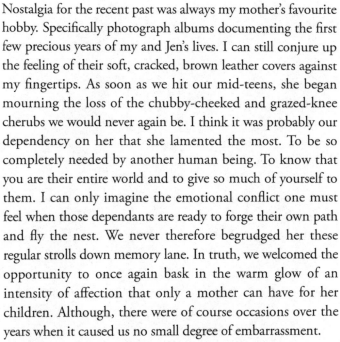

Nostalgia for the recent past was always my mother's favourite hobby. Specifically photograph albums documenting the first few precious years of my and Jen's lives. I can still conjure up the feeling of their soft, cracked, brown leather covers against my fingertips. As soon as we hit our mid-teens, she began mourning the loss of the chubby-cheeked and grazed-knee cherubs we would never again be. I think it was probably our dependency on her that she lamented the most. To be so completely needed by another human being. To know that you are their entire world and to give so much of yourself to them. I can only imagine the emotional conflict one must feel when those dependants are ready to forge their own path and fly the nest. We never therefore begrudged her these regular strolls down memory lane. In truth, we welcomed the opportunity to once again bask in the warm glow of an intensity of affection that only a mother can have for her children. Although, there were of course occasions over the years when it caused us no small degree of embarrassment.

One of the more memorable examples of this being the first time Jen brought a boyfriend back to the family home. She'd met Sean at college about six months earlier and had fallen head over heels for the bright-eyed, pointy-faced young slip of a boy. A spikey bedhead of bleached-blonde hair framing a slightly rat-like, although not unattractive, pasty face. He wore a sky-blue skater T-shirt with the word 'AD-DICT' inscribed across it. His ludicrously baggy jeans sagged below his backside to reveal a pair of bright-yellow boxers.

It's fair to say that my father wasn't instantly enamoured of him. Although I'm not sure that was ever a possibility, regardless of who had walked through the door. After a slightly awkward dinner we retired to the living room, cups of coffee in hand.

We'd barely sat down when my mother reached for the photo albums.

'Oh no, please, Mum ... not the albums.'

'Don't be so silly, Jen.'

'Sean doesn't want to see baby photos.'

'I would actually,' chipped in the young interloper with something of a wry smile as he avoided my sister's incredulous glare. Over the next thirty minutes or so, Jen was forced to endure the embarrassment of a scene played out in countless homes across the ages. The rest of us slowly but surely warmed to Sean as he laughed and fawned over the photographs in time with my mother. Jen standing proud beside her first bike or sat in her highchair covered in chocolate. Dressed as Doctor Who for the playschool fancy dress party or sat beside a sandcastle on a beach in Cornwall. And of course, most embarrassing of all, the obligatory naked in the bath shot that drew cries of, 'Oh God, Mum ... please no!'

As ever, my mother reacted to each photograph as though it were the first time she'd laid eyes on it. Every now and then, she'd point the album in my father's direction.

'Aw, just look at our girl.'

When they'd finally reached the end, Jen leapt up and grabbed the albums from the table.

'I'll put these away now!'

As she placed them back in the cupboard and out of sight, she called out, 'Hey, Mum, what are these?'

She pulled out two decidedly tatty-looking albums and held them aloft. My mother looked accusingly at my father.

'I thought I'd told you to put those back where you found them?'

My father was smiling broadly and looking particularly pleased with himself. 'Those are your mother's baby photos. I found them in the loft the other day. Bring them over, Jen.'

'Oh, now I'm sure nobody wants to see those old things,' my mother protested.

'We would actually.'

In fact, they weren't just baby photos but rather scrap books full of pictures, drawings and cuttings that charted my mother's life from babe-in-arms to trendy teenager.

'Why have we never seen these before?' Jen asked.

'They're your grandfather's really. I keep meaning to give them back to him but, well, they ended up in the loft. Which is where they should've stayed!' She looked at my father in mock exasperation.

My grandfather had recorded every significant moment in his daughter's young life. A painted handprint aged one, the date and time of her first steps. I noticed that my grandmother didn't appear in a single photograph and silently contemplated what that meant. The albums we were now fawning over must in effect be second editions. Updated versions with one of the main protagonists written out. I wondered to myself what his motivation for doing this had been and remembered what he had once told me about my mother's inability to come to terms with my grandmother leaving them. I suspected he'd painstakingly recreated these albums in an attempt to, in some way, give back to her the childhood memories she'd felt were lost to her. The fact that they'd ended up becoming permanent residents of the forgotten wasteland that was our loft strongly suggested that my grandfather's attempts had failed. My mother, I suspected, still felt the presence of the woman who abandoned her when she looked at these pictures.

I don't know if the others drew the same conclusions but, in any case, nobody mentioned the absent spectre that hung in the air as we studied with delight the images of a girl and young woman so vividly and spookily recognisable to us. We were full of questions about every aspect of the photos, from locations to fashion choices as well as the names of forgotten faces from chapters of a story we now understood we'd only begun reading part way through.

One picture in particular caught the attention of my sister, Sean and me. It was the very last photo in the albums and showed my mother at about fifteen. She wore flared trousers and a long suede shearling coat. Her curly dark hair, which we nearly always saw tied back, cascaded down past her shoulders. A cigarette hung from the corner of her mouth and she arched a provocative eyebrow at the camera.

'Wow, Mum, you were hot!' shrieked Jen.

'Yeah,' muttered Sean, instantly realising his mistake as Jen glared at him.

'And you're smoking!' I added with barely concealed relish.

My mother laughed and grabbed hold of the album to take a closer look. 'Your grandfather was so angry when he saw this picture. I was grounded and given a lecture on the dangers of smoking. I wonder why he kept it.'

I'd like to think that between us we helped my grandfather that day in his attempt to give my mother back some of the memories she'd cast aside. I don't think she allowed herself to be transported back exactly, but I believe that she took genuine pleasure at our interest in her past. Watching us study, with curiosity and love, the images of her growing up had mended, or perhaps finally extinguished something. In any event, the albums didn't go back in the loft but rather remained in the cupboard with the others, where they belonged.

≡

As I understand it, most people who have a midlife crisis buy a sports car, or have an affair or something. My father decided on a very different course of action.

'Your father wants to climb Kilimanjaro.'

'I'm sorry, say that again.'

'It's a mountain in Tasmania.'

'I know what it is, Mum ... and it's in Tanzania. What do you mean he wants to climb it?'

'Oh, I don't know what's the matter with him.'

'Nothing's the matter with me,' I just about heard my father call out from somewhere within earshot.

'Well, you've never wanted to climb a mountain before. You're nearly fifty, for goodness' sake.'

'When did this happen? What ... I mean, doesn't he have to train for it or...?'

'Oh, I don't know, love, I'll pass him the phone. You can try and talk some sense into him.'

I heard my mother's footsteps through the phone line and then her muffled words as she passed my father the receiver.

'Here you are, talk to your son and explain to him why you want to kill yourself in bloody Tasmania.'

'It's Tanzania ... hello?'

'Hi, Dad.'

'Hello, son, you okay?'

'Yeah, not bad cheers ... What's all this about Kilimanjaro?'

'It's a mountain in...'

'I know what it is, Dad! Since when are you interested in climbing a mountain?'

'Well … why not?'

I found it difficult to know how to respond to that. 'Well, what made you think of it? Don't you have to train for, like, months and stuff? It's going to be, well, y'know, really tough.'

'Well, I didn't think it would be easy, son. Give me some credit. And I'm booking it for next year, so I've got plenty of time to train.'

'Right. So you're serious then?'

'Absolutely. It's a once-in-a-lifetime opportunity.'

'It's a bit out of the blue.'

'No, it isn't.'

'Isn't it?'

'No.'

'I mean, you've literally never mentioned anything about mountains as long as I've been alive.'

'Well this is all very supportive, I must say. Is it too much to expect your family to get behind you when you tell them you want to climb a mountain? If you must know, I hurt my back while doing a bit of gardening.'

Amid his sighing, my father paused and I felt the need to goad him on. 'And…'

'And … I went to the doctors.'

'And he said you should climb Kilimanjaro?'

'It was a she actually.'

'Dad?!'

'Alright, alright. I went to the doctors and she told me I'm getting on a bit. Nothing wrong with me as such … just … Well, I mean my back's okay, got some pills. But she said I needed to start looking after myself. Exercising and all…'

'She probably meant go for a jog, not climb a…'

'Will you let me finish?'

'Sorry.'

'Anyway, it got me thinking. I mean, it came as a surprise, y'know? I've always been pretty active and, well, I don't think of myself as old.'

'Oh, Dad, you're not…'

'Will you let me finish?!'

'Sorry.'

'Then I bumped into John at the grocers and he told me about poor old Porky Smith…'

'Have you finished?'

'What? Oh, sorry. I went to school with him. Porky died last month of a heart attack. On top of everything else, it knocked me for six a bit. I mean, it could be me next.'

'Well, I mean, as you said, you're pretty active and, well, I don't want to be insensitive … but I'm going to assume you didn't call him Porky because he had a curly tail?'

'It's not just that. Seeing John again … it made me start thinking about, well, everything really. He looked so bloody old and tired. It seems like only yesterday he was a fresh-faced young newlywed. Time waits for no man and all that, son. I've got less in front of me now than behind me. And that's a bit scary.'

Hearing him speak like this terrified me. Apart from anything else, he never talked about his feelings so candidly. Plus, I'd never attached any particular age to either of my parents and the idea of them getting old had never really crossed my mind. I could feel a wave of panic creeping up inside me and fought to keep it at bay. My father was a racing driver. Big and strong and invincible. He can't be a fifty-year-old man with a bad back.

'So,' he continued, 'I just wanted to do something, y'-

know? Something new and exciting, while I still can. I'll never be Nigel Mansell now. I'll never fly to the moon or marry Twiggy.'

'Twiggy?'

'Because it's too late. I'll never be young again. But … it's not too late to climb a mountain.'

'Right … I see.' And I did. I didn't want to, but I did.

My father was a racing driver. Big and strong and invincible. My father was also a mountain climber. Ben Nevis to be specific. He never made it to Kilimanjaro. A few months after that phone conversation, he climbed the Scottish mountain in the depths of winter and, although he proclaimed to have loved every minute of it, it apparently relieved him of the need to climb the big one. 'Bugger that for a game of soldiers,' was his exact response when asked, as I recall. But he did take better care of himself from then on. Lots of hiking and cycling followed and succeeded in keeping him fit and healthy.

That phone call stayed with me always. Not just because it gave me the unwelcome realisation of my father's mortality and, to a lesser extent, vulnerability, but also because he was able to open up and share his concerns with me. It stands as a marker in our relationship. We'd come through my terrible teens and early twenties intact and were now re-establishing our bond. Stronger and closer than ever.

■

There are moments when I forget why I'm searching. When the darkness floods the empty space. But then I remember those eyes. I cling on to the sorrow and the embers of hope that flickered through the coldest night to light the way. Under the obscured moonlight, we are alone amid the churning, roaring decay. Two points, separate and still, as all around us race towards the fire. But we will be together when the night finally ends. When the sun rises on a new life and this place is no more than a fading dream whose details flutter away on the warm breeze.

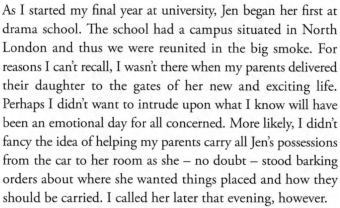

As I started my final year at university, Jen began her first at drama school. The school had a campus situated in North London and thus we were reunited in the big smoke. For reasons I can't recall, I wasn't there when my parents delivered their daughter to the gates of her new and exciting life. Perhaps I didn't want to intrude upon what I know will have been an emotional day for all concerned. More likely, I didn't fancy the idea of helping my parents carry all Jen's possessions from the car to her room as she – no doubt – stood barking orders about where she wanted things placed and how they should be carried. I called her later that evening, however.

As I'd expected, she was brimming with excitement as she enthusiastically told me about the other people in her building and her plans for her room. There was Rihanna, living across the corridor, who was very cool and wore a Rage Against the Machine T-shirt. There was Dave a few doors down with ginger hair and a real actual tattoo.

'I think he's gay, so you should meet him.'

I let that slide and continued to listen affectionately as she carried on with her stream of consciousness download. There was Vinit at the other end of the corridor who was a bit dishy, despite his bumfluff beard, and Martha next door who seemed a bit straight, but very nice anyway.

'We're all off out tonight, you should come along.'

'No thanks, sis. I remember what freshers' week is like and I only want to do that once. Besides, you don't want your older brother tagging along on your first night.'

'I keep telling you, it's not freshers' week. That's not how it's done here. But whatever, suit yourself. We should meet up soon though.'

Rolly, Tabitha, myself and our friend Sam had recently moved to a flat in Mornington Crescent and so I arranged to meet Jen that weekend and show her the unique and intoxicating delights of Camden Town.

Camden in the late nineties was a pulsing, throbbing mess of vibrant counter cultures. When walking along its bustling streets, you felt as though you were in the very epicentre of everything that mattered. A melting pot of nationalities, class and fashion. Crusties, ravers, metallers and indie kids. Tourists and lifers, the young and the younger. A potent bohemia that always had an undercurrent of danger. Men with darting eyes whispering, 'Hash, pills, coke? You want hash, pills, coke?' as they stood outside shops that sold 'I ❤ London' T-shirts and plastic Union Jack bowler hats. No matter what time of day or night, there would always be stumbling drunks and heavy-lidded stoners wandering among the blurry crowds. Endless colourful market stalls with knock-off Nirvana shirts, bongs, lava lamps and retro seventies clothing. The pungent aromatic smells of street food spanning the globe that hung heavy like low cloud over everything and everyone. In short, the ideal place to take your rookie sister when looking to impress her with your bona fide London credentials.

We met outside the crowded station and manoeuvred our way through the jostling masses beneath the heat of the midday sun. We passed a tall thin man painted silver and standing motionless like a statue, another wearing only a nappy and sucking on a dummy. A skin-headed woman in a Wu-Tang Clan hoody tried to sell us some skunk and a smiling man in a pinstripe suit handed us a leaflet advising us that our souls were damned for all eternity. By the bridge over the lock, a ghetto blaster pumped out Gabba techno as a drag queen and an elderly Rasta with long white dreadlocks danced in front of it. We ate vegetarian Chinese dumplings and washed them down with mango lassis. I played the part of the experienced patron to perfection as I guided my baby sister around the maze-like markets and sinewy side streets. Jen tried on all manner of clothes and jewellery and a pair of yellow rubber boots with six-inch spikey platform heels in the Cyberdog shop. I revelled in the opportunity to show off but was also just thrilled to be with Jen again. I'd missed her.

Eventually, we settled in a gloriously shabby pub just off the main thoroughfare. The entire establishment was covered from top to bottom in a layer of stickiness. Our shoes squelched on the discoloured faux-wooden flooring, and the concoction of stale beer and cigarette smoke permeated the air so thickly that you could almost take a bite. A terrified-looking teen was perched on the tiny stage in one corner, tuning an acoustic guitar, never daring to look up. The whole place was shrouded in darkness, despite the late summer sunshine beyond its four walls. We sat down on a wobbly table in the murkiest nook we could find. The frayed beer mats welded themselves to our pint glasses as we sipped our flat beers.

We ended up sitting in that spot far into the night, feasting on short-dated Golden Wonder crisps and slowly passing through tipsy to arrive at plain old drunk. The pub filled and emptied and filled again around us. The terrified teen played his set to an unadoring crowd. Nervous renditions of 'Fake Plastic Trees' and 'Hallelujah', interspersed with his own inexperienced but heartfelt odes to lost love and loneliness. The world around us babbled and sparked, rushed and slurred. But we didn't notice any of it.

We held each other's attention fully as we talked and laughed, sparred and teased. The comfort and closeness of our sibling bond infused with a new level of freedom and ferocity in deference to this new chapter in our combined story. Jen told me how emotional our parents had been when they said goodbye. How our father had fought to contain his outrage upon discovering that Jen's halls of residence weren't split into single sex dorms. We both descended into tipsy giggles as she recounted his furrowed brow and threatening stares when Vinit and Dave introduced themselves. She told me how our grandfather had arrived at our parents' house to wave her off, laden with a huge bag of pink and white marshmallows as a leaving gift. We reminisced, gossiped and planned.

She confided in me her fears for her relationship with Sean. He'd been getting increasingly jealous and possessive in the run-up to her leaving and had recently announced his intention to follow her to London.

'What, like some little lost sheep?'

'Oh, I don't know. He probably won't. I mean, he can't afford it. I miss him, of course. But ... he's, well ... so intense *all the time.*'

In retrospect, I should've picked up on this. Afforded it more significance. I don't think anyone could have foreseen what was to come, but it isn't true to say there weren't warning signs.

Jen told me that she and her best friend Anna, who was off to York University, had recorded mixtapes for each other as leaving presents and I told her that Rolly and I had done the same, in what now felt like another life. We then both failed to stifle our guffaws as she admitted that Anna's tape to her included more than one song by Savage Garden. She asked me how Rolly was and I told her he was doing great and that Tabitha – or Tabs – was lovely. And after all that, we just kept talking. About everything and nothing. The hours melted away until eventually we declared our shock as time was called at the bar. Where had the day gone?

Sometimes the most vivid memories aren't those linked to a significant event. Every detail of that precious day is recorded in my mind to be replayed as and when required. My baby sister, with whom I would so often stroll along the silent Mill Lane beneath the moon and stars, now walked beside me down the bustling streets of Camden in the neon glow of the night. The little girl with the Sunshine Bear and the boy who peed in her toyboxes. From BMXs in the back garden to beers in the big smoke. We were reunited and London was our oyster. Over the next three years or so, until I left the capital, Jen and I met up regularly and created many more memories that would further strengthen our already unbreakable bond.

■

I dream of finding you dead. A rotting carcass, emaciated and discarded. Unrecognisable among the festering debris of inevitability. I dream of never finding you. Of listlessness swallowing the city. But at least I dream.

As I scan and trawl, rummage and scratch, I dream again. A slumbering, slobbering wretch with no shadow. Forward, onward into this everlasting night. I dream again of a place beyond the numbness. I dream of finding you when I am dead. Too late.

≡

The end of the century. The end of the decade that culturally defined us. A new millennium that coincided with the conclusion of my and Rolly's academic lives. Beyond the Y2K bugs and doomsday prophecies, serious adulthood awaited us. With its careers and responsibilities. Its rents and mortgages, electricity bills and tax returns. Its pasta bakes and sensible shoes, daily commutes and Sunday papers. A truly terrifying prospect for both of us. We'd just graduated and both received a 2:1 in our respective fields, a grade that came as a pleasant surprise for me and a slight disappointment for Rolly.

'It doesn't even have its own slang term.'

'What do you mean?'

'Well, a first is a Geoff, right?'

'Hirst?'

'Exactly. A 2:2 is a Desmond.'

'Tutu?'

'Yep. And a third is a Thora.'

'I thought it was a Douglas?'

'Well, whatever. A 2:1 hasn't even got *anything*, mate.'

Tabs had got a first in English Literature and wasn't wasting a single opportunity to point out to Rolly that this clearly meant that she was the intellectual half of the partnership.

As the end of the world loomed, there seemed only one reasonable course of action open to us: throw a party.

Not just any party though. A party to end all others. A get-together worthy of a once-in-a-lifetime occasion. A celebration of youth in the face of its passing. The three of us duly set about organising the event under the weight of understanding that it needed to be a night that everyone attending would remember for the rest of their lives. It very quickly became clear that our boxy student flat was not up to the challenge. Likewise, the guestlist soon grew well beyond the capacity of a house party. Old friends from back home were added to the list of uni friends and then expanded to include partners. Eventually the party morphed into a getaway and we booked three large cottages on the Devon coast. Side by side but otherwise isolated from the rest of the world. It cost a fortune, with the bill being almost exclusively footed by Tabs.

Friends were contacted, supplies were bought, scored and acquired. Everyone on my list could make it with the exception of Jen, who was seeing New Year in around at Sean's. A fact that, if I didn't know better, I'd say she didn't sound too happy about. In the end, twenty-seven of us descended on a remote stretch of West Country coastline on 30th December 1999. Rolly and I travelled with Tabs and her friend Lou. Had our car been stopped by the police en route, we could all have expected prison sentences for dealing drugs, as we brazenly carried with us baggies of pills, coke and weed to supply the entire party.

What followed were three days and nights of non-stop hedonism. The world was changing and so were we. But not without a fight. Twenty-four seven the party raged, across all three cottages. Sex, drugs and … well, indie music mainly. Although one of the cottages, inhabited predominantly by Tabs' friends from back home, blasted out thumping drum and bass around the clock. I remember wandering from scene to scene and buzz to buzz. Garbled, senseless conversations and fumbling tactile encounters. The rush of coming up, the slow-witted drag of a joint and the arrogant roar of a snorted line. Stolen moments of sleep that wasn't really sleep, propped against a wall or bony shoulder. Traces of light, echoes of laughter and losing grip on the edge of mania.

When midnight on the 31st came around, I think half of the partygoers probably missed it entirely. I, however, happened to be in a room where a couple of very stoned uni mates were sat with their faces an inch from a television screen. They suddenly began shouting the countdown from ten, nine, eight and, by six, the whole room was yelling in wasted harmony. Rolly and Tabs appeared beside me – or perhaps they'd always been there – and the three of us embraced as the nation erupted into cheers. I turned to face the best friend I'd ever had and said what I thought he needed to hear at this momentous moment in our lives.

'It's called an Attila.'

'What?'

'Attila the Hun … 2:1.'

Early on the morning of the 2nd of January in the year 2000, all three cottages sat silent for the first time since we'd arrived. Rolly gently shook me awake and whispered, 'Come on, get up, we're going for a walk.'

For reasons I couldn't fathom, we gingerly picked our way through the sleeping bodies and out into the cold coastal winds of the twenty-first century.

'What's going on, Rolly?'

'Come on, let's walk.'

We wandered along the muddy coastal path scorched along the edge of the clifftops. The sea was furious. It growled and spat many feet below us. My trainers were covered in mud and I began to whine and moan like a child.

'Okay, this'll do.'

He turned to me and the serious look on his face suddenly morphed into a familiar broad smile.

'What on earth are you smiling about, you utter shit? I'm freezing my arse off here.'

'I've asked Tabs to marry me, mate.'

I stared at him, slack-jawed for just a few seconds, and then threw my arms around him as I broke into joyful laughter.

'She said yes! I wanted you to be the first to know.'

'Mate, that's absolutely fucking fantastic.'

'You'll be my best man?'

I remember feeling an elation at that moment that was far beyond any artificial high. This brave new dawn suddenly seemed something to be embraced, not anything to run away from. Yes, everything was changing … the nineties were over. The party was at an end. But so what? We were ready for whatever came next. The next chapter appeared all at once to be full of wonderous possibilities.

'But there's a problem.'

'What?'

'There's a reason she maybe should've said no … in fact, there's a reason that even asking her might have been a really fucked up thing to do.'

'Mate, you two are meant to be together. Whatever it is I'm sure–'

'I'm dying.'

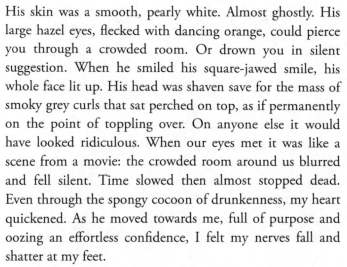

His skin was a smooth, pearly white. Almost ghostly. His large hazel eyes, flecked with dancing orange, could pierce you through a crowded room. Or drown you in silent suggestion. When he smiled his square-jawed smile, his whole face lit up. His head was shaven save for the mass of smoky grey curls that sat perched on top, as if permanently on the point of toppling over. On anyone else it would have looked ridiculous. When our eyes met it was like a scene from a movie: the crowded room around us blurred and fell silent. Time slowed then almost stopped dead. Even through the spongy cocoon of drunkenness, my heart quickened. As he moved towards me, full of purpose and oozing an effortless confidence, I felt my nerves fall and shatter at my feet.

'Hello, you look as though you could do with a drink?'

And I could. Of course I could. I'd done nothing but drink for the last three weeks. I was still not dealing with recent events. I hadn't stepped up to the plate when called upon or been the rock my friend so needed me to be. In fact, I'd ejected myself from life and found myself a hole to wallow in. Festering in my own self-pity.

'I'm not good company right now.'

'That's alright. I am. So, between us we'll be fine.'

I smiled at this. The first in a long time. Then I allowed him to buy me a drink and join me in my self-indulgent little grief corner. Over the next few hours we talked both at and with each other. He soon understood that this would not be the flirtatious dance he'd been looking for. No coquettish back and forth was to be had. Yet, instead of backing off once he'd come to realise this, he stayed. He listened to my half-cut lamentations and didn't simply offer a series of sympathetic platitudes, but instead weighed in as though we were trusted old friends. As though our relationship had already been shaped and our respective roles within it long since determined.

It was not all one way either. As the night wore on, he revealed himself to me in a manner that felt both frighteningly exciting and entirely natural. Born and raised on the south coast, he came to London to study six years ago and decided to stay on after he'd graduated.

'I don't think I could ever leave now. The city is in my blood. If there's no tube stop there, I'm not interested.'

He was a few years my senior and his extra life experience must have been equally evident to both of us. He was a social creature. Well-spoken and radiating self-assuredness. His stories took place in fashionable clubs and at exclusive after-show parties. Drug-fuelled tales that dripped with excitement but hinted at his desire for something more tangible and real. I found it impossible not to fall head over heels. His company was intoxicating. For a few dreamy hours my burden was relieved. There was only him, his white-toothed smile and dark swirling eyes.

'Aren't you a bit young to have gone grey?'

He laughed at this. A sweet, open-mouthed giggle that hinted at an innocence beyond the pouting swagger.

'Aren't you a bit young to be carrying the weight of the world?' he replied.

We went back to his that night. To the flat above the greasy spoon where we'd eat breakfast the following morning. And many more mornings over the next two years. To the flat I would move into just two dizzying months later. With the view of the bustling London high street that I'd spend endless hours gazing down at. Watching life unfold. To the flat that would be the setting for a new life. My new life.

X

'What do I need to do to make that happen?'

'Well, you could start by telling me your name?'

'I ... I don't want anyone to ... not yet.'

'Okay, no problem. Let's start with something easier, shall we? Do you remember how you got here?'

'I was beaten up.'

'Do you know who by?'

'No. Just some ... I stopped them ... Oh God, are you sure he's okay?'

'I promise you he's doing fine. What about before that? Do you live in London?'

'No, Bristol.'

'So, you're not homeless?'

'No.'

'And there's family or friends in Bristol who may be looking for you?'

'There's one. Maybe. But she ... It depends how long I've been ... when can I see him?'

'Well, at the moment, neither of you are well enough. But in a few days, maybe. This ... relative? Partner? In Bristol, we could call her for you, if you...'

'No ... I don't know. Please, I'm very tired.'

'What's her name?'

PART TWO

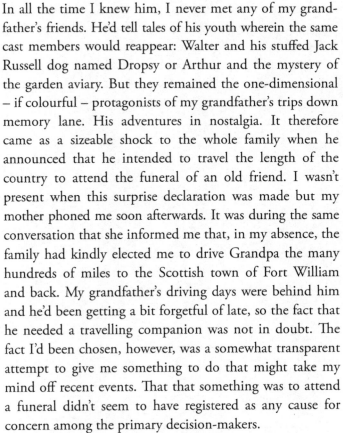

In all the time I knew him, I never met any of my grand-father's friends. He'd tell tales of his youth wherein the same cast members would reappear: Walter and his stuffed Jack Russell dog named Dropsy or Arthur and the mystery of the garden aviary. But they remained the one-dimensional – if colourful – protagonists of my grandfather's trips down memory lane. His adventures in nostalgia. It therefore came as a sizeable shock to the whole family when he announced that he intended to travel the length of the country to attend the funeral of an old friend. I wasn't present when this surprise declaration was made but my mother phoned me soon afterwards. It was during the same conversation that she informed me that, in my absence, the family had kindly elected me to drive Grandpa the many hundreds of miles to the Scottish town of Fort William and back. My grandfather's driving days were behind him and he'd been getting a bit forgetful of late, so the fact that he needed a travelling companion was not in doubt. The fact I'd been chosen, however, was a somewhat transparent attempt to give me something to do that might take my mind off recent events. That that something was to attend a funeral didn't seem to have registered as any cause for concern among the primary decision-makers.

And so it was that my grandfather and I climbed into my father's ailing old Ford Orion one freezing February morning and set off for bonny Scotland. We'd never had any trouble sustaining a conversation, the two of us would chat endlessly on the phone at least once a week and in person whenever we could, so the prospect of being trapped in an enclosed space together for hours on end was of no concern to either of us. Sure enough, in no time at all, the radio was muted and we were in full swing. Updates on the family and current affairs commentaries were seamlessly interspersed with rounds of twenty questions and I spy. The first few hours flew by. Then – inevitably – the conversation turned to the matter at hand.

'So, tell me about this friend of yours who we're driving halfway round the world for then, Grandpa. Jack, right?'

'Ha … Jack. Dear old Jack. He was a canny lad was Jack. Big heart, small brain.'

'I'm not sure I've heard you mention him before?'

'No, probably not. We weren't that close.'

'Erm, right. So why are we … I mean…'

'You mean why are we driving to Scotland to go to the funeral of someone you've never heard of and I haven't seen in over fifty years?'

'Well … yes.'

There was a long pause before my grandfather let out a quiet sigh. 'Because he's the last.'

'The last what?'

'The last of the old gang.'

I was momentarily taken aback by this.

'Yep, when old Jack is six feet under, there's only me left. The old Totnes Terrors are no more.'

'The old what?'

'That's what Arthur's mum used to call us. It just kind of stuck. Not that we were terrorisers of course. A lovelier group of boys you couldn't hope to find. Sure, we got ourselves in a few scrapes but they were all decent honest lads. No … I have to be there to see him off. Nothing else for it.'

For the first time that I could remember, the conversation between us faltered. I didn't know what to say. I had so many questions but for some reason I found that I wasn't able to ask them.

After a brief silence I changed the subject. 'So, what brought him to Scotland?'

'He married a young lass by the name of ... should all that smoke be there?' He pointed to the front of the car, where plumes of white smoke were rising from the bonnet.

'Oh sh—'

'Best pull her over, my boy.'

For the next forty minutes we stood shivering on the frozen banks of the M6 until, eventually, the breakdown truck appeared. It was driven by a wiry man with more than a passing resemblance to Shakin' Stevens.

'Nah, it's knackered,' he said, after spending all of thirty seconds with his head under the bonnet. 'Nothing I can do for you here. Where's home?'

'Just outside Bristol,' replied my grandfather.

Shakin' Stevens whistled. 'Where you going?'

'Fort William,' I said. Shakin' Stevens frowned. 'In Scotland,' I added.

Shakin' Stevens whistled again. 'Well, I can get you to Stoke.'

'Stoke?!'

'Yep. I'll get you to a garage, see if they can mend this old thing for you. That's the best I can do.'

An hour or so later we found ourselves standing shivering again, this time outside a garage in Stoke-on-Trent, waiting for the verdict. Shakin' Stevens had long since driven off behind the green door of his tow truck, wishing us luck getting to 'Port William' as he departed.

'Do you know what the word Stoke means?' my grandfather queried, with a cheerful lack of appreciation regards the magnitude of the situation. Whether this question was directed towards me or the mechanic assessing the damage, I'm unsure. In any case, neither of us answered so he continued, unperturbed: 'It's the word for a small village or settlement that's dependent on a larger town or settlement for its existence.'

I looked at him. 'Where's Stoke-on-Trent dependent on then?'

He paused as if in contemplation. 'Don't know.'

'Nah, it's knackered,' cut in the mechanic. 'Head gasket. I can get you a new one fitted but it won't be today. And, to be honest, it'll cost you more than the car's worth.'

I swore and looked at my grandfather, who appeared to be rummaging around in his pockets.

'Marshmallow?' he enquired.

I told the mechanic we'd need to speak to my parents and would get back to him. Suddenly I was in a panic. It felt to me at that moment like the final straw. The ailing camel's back was finally broken. A sense of chaos threatened to engulf me and it seemed as though my life was spiralling out of control. I had no job, no future and no clue what to do next...

'I've never been to Stoke before,' my grandfather said. I'd let down my best friend when he needed me the most and now I was stranded in Stoke-on-Trent. I began to swear under my breath and put my head in my hands.

'You know who would have found this funny?' he added, calmly. I didn't answer him. 'Jack.'

I looked at him then, suddenly remembering why we were here in the first place.

'Oh, Grandpa! The funeral ... we're not going to make it!

I'm so sor–'

Then he started laughing. First a gravelly chuckle and then a hearty guffaw that brought tears to his eyes. 'He'd have absolutely loved this! They all would!'

I smiled at him as he bent double with laughter and before I knew it, I was laughing with him.

'Silly Old Peaty Doubler, stranded in bloody Stoke of all places. They'll all be looking down at me, well-nigh wetting themselves.'

'Pete who?'

'Come on, let's go find something to eat and I'll tell you all about it. Here, can we go to one of those slushy places that everyone's talking about?'

After some deliberation, we agreed that what he meant was sushi. I'd never tried it myself and, in truth, wasn't especially keen to. I tried to put him off the idea but to no avail.

'You know it's raw fish, right?'

'That's the one!'

'Are you sure?'

'Course I am … I'm on a roll here. You don't get too many first times when you're my age. First time in Stoke, first time eating slushy.'

'Well, when in Stoke, I suppose.'

Sushi restaurants were two a penny in London by this point and not too difficult to find in Bristol either. In Stoke, however … but eventually we did find one in a shiny indoor shopping centre called The Potteries. Watching my grandfather eat raw tuna for the first time is something that has stayed with me. But then that whole night has stayed with me. From minor disaster came a shared experience that simply couldn't have happened under any other circumstances.

'So, when it was my round I'd always stick to the ale, you

see? Cheap, watered down stuff it was in them days. But it did the trick. Then when it was Jack's or Walt's, or anyone else's round I'd say: "Mine's a whisky. Single malt, make it a double, something peaty."'

'I've never had a proper single malt whisky.'

'What?! Good Lord, my boy. You haven't lived. Well, let's go and put that right, shall we?'

And so the day of firsts continued. As the sun set, I found myself in a pub in Stoke-on-Trent sipping peaty single malt whisky with Old Peaty Doubler himself.

'I like it.'

'Course you do, it's in the blood, my boy.'

Over the course of the next few hours we got drunk together, which was another first for both of us. We'd been a bit tipsy in front of each other at Christmas over the years but we were now entering the realms of fully sozzled. My grandfather told me tales of the Totnes Terrors and I listened attentively, completely enthralled. Stories of racing motor-bikes down country lanes and squabbling over the affections of farmers' daughters. Young boys growing into young men who eventually drifted apart. The timing was not lost on me, a fact I'm sure my grandfather was fully aware of.

'They were some of the best times of my life and I'll remember them till the day I die, for sure. But only *some* of the best times, my boy. Only some. There's love, family … most of all family. Your mum, you and Jen. Life is beautiful, never forget that. It'll kick you in the teeth from time to time … but it's always beautiful. Sometimes the beauty is in the changes.'

We raised a glass or three to Jack and all the lads of the Totnes Terrors. Then, at some point many hours into the evening, I remembered something.

'The car!'

We once again descended into giggles and then belly laughs. We managed to find a hotel in the city centre and in the morning, we were both very much the worse for wear. The first and last hangover I ever shared with my grandfather. We spoke to my parents and sorted everything out. My father, much to his chagrin, was forced to pay for the stricken vehicle to be towed to its final resting place. I can't remember where the blame for the whole sorry escapade landed in the end, though it really doesn't matter; it was only a car after all. We never got to the funeral but somehow my grandfather had done what he'd set out to do. He'd paid his respects to Jack. The last of the Totnes Terrors and his grandson made their way home on a coach.

≡

'Well, come on then, tell me all about him.'

'What do you want to know, Mum?'

'Well, his name would be a start.'

'It's Leon.'

'Ooh, that's a bit different, isn't it?'

'Is it?'

'And what does Leon do?'

'He's a promotor.'

'I see ... what does he promote?'

'Erm, I don't really know. Events and stuff.'

'Ooh, sounds clever.'

'I suppose.'

'And does he look like Lister from *Red Dwarf*?'

'What?!'

'Now, I may be wrong, but I've always thought you may have carried a torch for that Lister.'

'Carried a torch ... Lister, really?'

'Anyway, most importantly of all, when do I get to meet him?'

'Ah, well, it's very early days, Mum. I mean we should probably give it another month or two at least.'

Silence followed.

'Mum?'

Still no answer came.

'Mum, you still there?'

'Right then ... sorry, I was just grabbing the calendar. Now then, we can do this Sunday. That'll give me time to get to my hairdressers.'

'Your hairdressers?! Mum, there's no need to…'

'Shall I pencil you both in?'

A few days later I found myself with sweaty palms as Leon and I pulled into my parents' driveway. I'm sure I caught a brief glimpse of my mother peering out of the upstairs window in anticipation as we arrived, like Jimmy Stewart in *Rear Window* but without the camera … hopefully.

'So, again, I'm really sorry about this. I know it's way too soo–'

'Will you stop apologising? I keep telling you it's fine. I'm looking forward to meeting them. Just as long as I'm not subjected to hours of baby photos or something!'

'Ha ha, yeah … right.'

It was my father who opened the door, with a strange look on his face that I didn't recognise. We hugged and he offered Leon his hand. We were launching into our hellos and nice to meet yous when my father grabbed my arm and whispered, 'Right … erm, your mother. There's been a bit of a … look, just don't say anything, okay? Act like you haven't noticed anything strange at all, okay?'

My mother then appeared from the stairway wearing a nervous smile. She'd dressed up for the occasion in a new dress and … hat. A big blue woolly hat.

'Hello, my lovely boy,' she said as she pulled me into a hug before turning to Leon, 'and you must be Leon.' They hugged and then my mother mumbled something about needing to check on the dinner and scurried off.

My first thought was a dark one. A completely illogical dark one as I'd only seen her a week ago. I turned to my father and urgently whispered: 'What's going on? Is she ill?

Is it…?'

'No, no … nothing like that, son. She couldn't get an appointment so she … look, I'll explain if I can later, but just keep schtum, alright?'

We hardly saw my mother over the next fifteen minutes or so, until we were all eventually seated round the dinner table. My father was left to awkwardly play the host in the meantime, as my mother – very obviously – pretended to be looking after the dinner. I tried on several occasions to get the truth from him but he just shushed me, pointing towards the kitchen in a panic as though my mother could hear every word.

She was still wearing the hat as she sat down at the table.

'Mum, I've got to–'

'Can you pass the potatoes please, son?' my father cut in through gritted teeth, his eyes widened in alarm, but I wouldn't be diverted.

'What's with the hat?'

A very long pause followed wherein my father's eyes darted rapidly back and forth between all of us. Each time they landed on me, he creased his brow to signify his anger at me, but he got muddled at some point and ended up looking angrily at Leon instead. After what felt like an age, my mother let out a long sigh of defeat. She slumped back in her chair and pulled the woolly hat from her head to reveal a tangled mop of bleached-blonde so bright that it was almost white. Bits of different length hair were sticking up at strange angles and her fringe looked as though it had been shaped using a pair of blunt gardening shears.

'Cool hair,' said Leon.

My mother's face fell but as she looked up at him, she realised that he wasn't mocking her but instead gazing at her in genuine appreciation. My mother had been a bottle blonde for a few years by this point, for some reason deciding to make the change when her natural black waves began to grey. She'd never previously attempted to apply it herself, though. The reasons for this now seemed pretty clear to me. Something had obviously gone very awry.

'I couldn't get an appointment at my hairdressers, you see. He was all booked up and I so wanted ... well, anyway, he told me the brand he uses so I thought ... well, I just thought ... the chemists say they can't ... well, it doesn't matter. The thing is, I didn't–'

'You didn't read the instructions,' chipped in my father, although the worried face he pulled immediately afterwards suggested that he wasn't fully aware that he'd been speaking out loud.

'Yes, dear, thank you. I didn't read the instructions and, well, you can see what happened. I thought if I tried to cut it back a bit it might ... I'm mortified!'

'It's looks awesome,' offered Leon. And, actually, looking at her again, he wasn't wrong. My mother looked kind of, well, cool.

'It's true, Mum. You look really grungy. And younger. It's great.'

'Well, it's very nice of you boys to say so. Your father said I look like Andy Warhol.' All eyes turned towards my father, who suddenly resembled a rabbit in the headlights.

'Potatoes ... pass them, *please*, son.'

The rest of the afternoon passed without major incident. My mother and Leon hit it off remarkably, despite a slightly odd moment when she observed that he didn't look very much like Lister from *Red Dwarf*. They discovered a mutual love of David Bowie and, bizarrely, a shared obsession with the ghost stories of MR James. Bizarre firstly because it's something I didn't know about either of them and secondly because I have no idea how they managed to get on to that subject during the course of the afternoon. Leon was indeed subjected to the mountain of baby photos (in fact, it looked very much to me as though my mother had marked the pages in the albums that contained the photos she'd wanted to show him in advance) but, in truth, he seemed to rather enjoy it. As with Sean's visit, my father and I were somewhat side-lined for most of the afternoon.

It dawned on me at some point, as I watched the two of them pawing over the photographs, that I felt an enormous sense of pride. Not in the pictures of me as a baby, and not towards Leon either, for so deftly impressing my mother and fitting in so comfortably and seamlessly. I felt a deep and almost overwhelming pride in my mother. Leon was right, she was cool. Everybody we brought home struck an instant rapport with her. In fact, almost everyone she met seemed to. As strange as it may seem, that moment was the first time I'd really acknowledged that. It wasn't that Leon was putting on a great performance upon meeting the other half's parents for the first time, or that Sean had done so before him. It was simply that my mum was great. They'd both instantly loved her and been made to feel at home by her. All of a sudden it wasn't me presenting Leon to my parents, or my mother showing off pictures of her baby boy to the newcomer. It was me showing off my mum. This is my mother. Yes, she is wonderful, actually, and you're lucky to have met her.

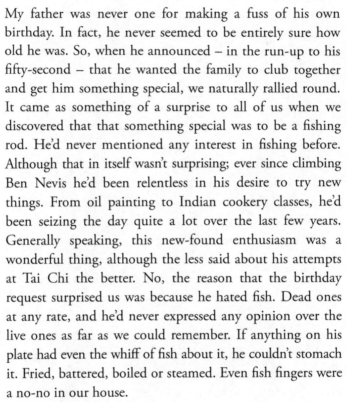

My father was never one for making a fuss of his own birthday. In fact, he never seemed to be entirely sure how old he was. So, when he announced – in the run-up to his fifty-second – that he wanted the family to club together and get him something special, we naturally rallied round. It came as something of a surprise to all of us when we discovered that that something special was to be a fishing rod. He'd never mentioned any interest in fishing before. Although that in itself wasn't surprising; ever since climbing Ben Nevis he'd been relentless in his desire to try new things. From oil painting to Indian cookery classes, he'd been seizing the day quite a lot over the last few years. Generally speaking, this new-found enthusiasm was a wonderful thing, although the less said about his attempts at Tai Chi the better. No, the reason that the birthday request surprised us was because he hated fish. Dead ones at any rate, and he'd never expressed any opinion over the live ones as far as we could remember. If anything on his plate had even the whiff of fish about it, he couldn't stomach it. Fried, battered, boiled or steamed. Even fish fingers were a no-no in our house.

Still, a fishing rod he wanted and a fishing rod we got him. As was usually the case with these fleeting but all-consuming interests, he spent the next few months deep in study, learning everything there was to learn about the noble art of fishing. Books and DVDs were practically inhaled in his desire to know all there was to know about his new favourite thing in the world. Even the vegetable patch went unattended for a few weeks. In terms of actually doing any fishing, things moved along a touch more slowly. If there was a secondary reason that this sudden interest might be surprising to the rest of the family, it was that he didn't really live anywhere near water. Much to my mother's embarrassment, this last fact led to him, on more than one occasion, taking his rod to the village green to practise casting. There he'd stand for hours on end, contented as can be, casting the line out among the beds of daffodils and dog poo bins. Cars would slow to observe the spectacle and parents would usher their children away from the strange man fishing on dry land.

Then one morning he called me and invited me to join him on a weekend trip he had planned to the Cornish coast. I had no interest in fishing, but I didn't hesitate. A chance to spend some time with the old man, father and son, like the old days, was too good to miss. On the drive down to the coast and the wonderfully named Crackington Haven, the talk was mainly of fish. Apparently, the spot we were heading for was prime fishing for mackerel, flat fish and whiting, whatever that was. As we drove down ever smaller country lanes and the scenery grew steadily more rural, his excitement at what lay ahead visibly increased. And when we got that first view of the sea on the horizon ahead, his enthusiasm spread to me and we both let out a 'woohoo' in unison.

Crackington Haven consisted of a few houses, a pub and a tiny picturesque beach flanked by two vast rocky hillsides. As we parked the car on the side of the road, a thought occurred to me, a thought that really should have occurred to me a good deal sooner. As this was a weekend trip, where would we be staying the night? A wave of fear washed over me as I imagined my father and I sharing a hastily constructed tent on a cold windswept cliff edge. Then my mind leapt to news reports of a missing father and son, with pictures of our faces on-screen as the newsreader gravely relayed details of our last known whereabouts and reminded the viewers of the dangers lying in wait when inexperience and the jagged British coastline collide. I bet myself that my mother would give them the photograph of me at my graduation, where I looked cross-eyed and chinless.

'Dad, we're not camping, are we?!'

'Course we are, son. Only way to do it properly.'

'But … but I…'

Then I noticed the mocking grin. 'We're staying in the pub.'

'Oh, thank God.'

We checked in to the pub, dumped our bags in our room and headed straight out for the sea.

'So, you've only got the one fishing rod, right?'

'Yep.'

'Right. So, what am I going to do for the next two days?'

'You're my helper.'

Visions of endless afternoons stood holding bulbs and seeds as my father tended his vegetable garden, or oily rags as he worked on the car, flashed before my eyes. As it turned out though, you're not really doing much when you're fishing anyway. He spent the first thirty minutes or so inspecting at close quarters what all the other folks fishing were up to. He would wander up to someone and study their bait and tackle and whatever else it is that you take fishing with you. Sometimes he'd casually enquire as to the extent of their catch today; other times he'd just stare for a bit, then wander off. We found a spot that – to my untrained eye – looked pretty much like every other spot. My father then did some very unappealing things to some unfortunate worm-like creatures and proceeded to put all those hours of training on the village green to the test by casting off.

And that was that. Then we just … stood. After about twenty minutes, my father turned to me and enquired, 'You want a go?'

'Nah.'

And then we stood some more.

As the afternoon meandered along, I could sense a quietly growing frustration in my father. Occasionally someone nearby would catch something and he would, almost in-audibly, tut or exhale. As his sense of disillusionment took root, our rod remaining determinedly motionless throughout, the conversation all but dried up. Gradually the afternoon light began to dull and the other fishermen and women started to pack up and head home. By this point I'd counted every pebble on the beach and pondered the futility of human existence until I could ponder no more. My father stood resolute, staring out to sea.

'Pub?' I ventured.

His shoulders fell slightly and he let out one last exhale. 'Yep.'

We ordered a couple of beers and the barman chipperly enquired as to whether we'd had many good catches this afternoon. I played along as my father explained to the fellow that the afternoon had been about as he expected. Ups and downs. And besides, he was really there for the ambience, you know? We sat on a bench outside as small groups of people gathered, drinks in hand, to watch the orange sunset.

After a few minutes silently sipping our drinks, my father smiled at me. 'So, fishing's a bit bloody boring, eh?'

I laughed and gestured towards the gently lapping waves. 'Still, this is all pretty amazing.'

'You're not wrong, son, you're not wrong.'

We didn't move from that spot until well into the night. Eating our dinner there, watching the sunset and talking endlessly. My father told me all about his adventures and misadventures in recent times.

This included the truth about his ill-fated attempts at Tai Chi that he'd omitted in all previous retellings. 'The problem was, I kept farting.'

I nearly choked on my beer at this and we both laughed.

'It can be very … relaxing, you see? The old muscles are doing things they're not used to and … I mean, if anything, I'm lucky I didn't follow through.' This was too much for me and I spilt my beer over myself as I collapsed into guffaws of laughter.

The remainder of the worm-like creatures were spared the next day. Instead of standing on the beach for hours on end and catching no fish, we went to nearby Tintagel to visit the seat of King Arthur. We ate ice creams and wandered along the stunning cliff edge as the sea elegantly swayed below us. We had fun. We made each other laugh and, in contrast to the previous afternoon, the time flew by. It was an occasion that cemented our friendship. We weren't just a father and son bonding and we didn't use the opportunity to have deep and meaningful conversations about each other's lives. No pearls of wisdom were handed down that day. He'd given me enough guidance in life and while he'd always be my father, my teacher and my childhood hero, he was now also my friend.

■

Beneath and to the right of the flickering light, just inside the safety of shadow, there is a blanket. It sits forgotten atop a flattened box that once had a purpose of its own. I sit, obscuring what remains of its worn and faded logo. I pull the blanket over myself. It is cold in a way that makes it seem damp. I shiver in the darkness beyond the flickering light. I try to find a position that might eventually lead to something like sleep. I think that it would not be so bad if I didn't wake up.

I have torn this city asunder. You are gone. I have scorched the boundaries of this broken Babylon. I have scaled its sullied heights and plumbed its lonely depths. You are gone. As is my heart now. I dared to think, to question. I'm no longer sure if I really saw you. Those eyes, that moment. You are gone. I think that it would not be so bad if I didn't wake up.

≡

When Jen phoned me that fateful evening, it was the first spring of the new millennium and my mind was elsewhere. I'd just moved in with Leon and, in part buoyed by this, was finding a way of coming to terms with my best friend's news. My thoughts were on the future. A new chapter. When I heard her broken voice quietly pleading down the phoneline though, everything changed.

'Jen? What is it?'

'Can you come, please. I ... please just come.'

'I'm on my way.'

About an hour later I was rapping frantically on the door of her room in her student halls of residence.

'Who's there?' she asked, sounding terrified.

'It's me.'

She opened the door and I nearly gasped out loud. She was as pale as a ghost except for her eyes, which were red raw from crying. She wore tatty old pyjamas and her fists were clenched and shaking. In fact, all of her was shaking. Her face wore a manic, desperate expression that I couldn't read.

'What's happened?'

She fell to the floor and began a terrifying mixture of sobs and breathless rasps for air. I ran to her side and held her, all the while asking again and again what was happening. After a few minutes her breathing slowed and she told me.

'Abortion, I've had an abortion.'

'What do you ... when?'

'Now. Today.'

'I don't … where's Sean?'

She looked at me with a sadness so heavy it almost crushed me. She told me everything then. Her relationship with Sean had been getting increasingly strained and troubling over the last six months or so. He had been getting more and more possessive and paranoid. Jealous of her friends and unpredictably moody. He'd try and control who she saw, where she went and what she wore.

'It was like he was possessed or something. Just suddenly out of nowhere he'd get angry. He'd get so pissed off over nothing.'

'Did he touch you? I mean, hit you or hurt you?'

'No, no … not physically. He'd just … it's difficult to explain, you know? He just wouldn't let me do anything… be myself.'

She explained how she'd tried to finish it with him shortly after she'd left home for college, but he'd begged her not to end it. He'd tried to move to London himself but couldn't afford to and so instead he'd just stay in Jen's room for days, sometimes weeks at a time. The two of them in that confined space.

'He never wanted to go out, always wanted us just to stay in. If we went out, even just to the shop or something, he'd accuse me of looking at other men all the time. It was so fucked up. He just kept getting worse until we basically never left the room while he was here.'

'Jesus, Jen, I'm so sorry. I should've–'

'Then, a month or so ago he started talking about marriage and kids. I freaked out and told him I wasn't ready for any of that, no way. But he just kept on and on about it. Saying if I loved him, I'd want to marry him now and have a family.' She started crying again and I held her in my arms. 'Then I missed my period. I just knew I was pregnant, I fucking knew it. And he must've, I mean we always used a condom.'

'You think he, what, split it deliberately or something?'

'I fucking know he did … I fucking know it.'

'So, did you tell him? I mean, does he know you got pregnant?'

'Yes, he found out. I don't even know how but he knew. I told him I had to get an abortion, I'm too young, I can't do this. He freaked, went mental. First, he just begged me to keep it. Pleaded with me. He was in tears, manic and out of control. Then when I wouldn't back down, he said he'd kill himself if I did it. If I killed our baby, I'd have to live with killing him as well.'

'Fucking bastard!'

'He doesn't know. That I've done it, I mean. I didn't tell him. I arranged it without him knowing and went today. I thought I could just say I miscarried or something but it was … it was worse than I … it was fucking awful, it was so fucking awful.'

She broke down again and I held her more tightly.

'It's okay … it's okay. I've got you, sis, I've got you.'

It wasn't okay, of course. It would never be okay. But the next twenty-four hours would at least see steps taken to remove Sean from Jen's life. My first call was to my parents. It had to be. They were everything they needed to be. Furious but focused. Determined to act immediately to protect their daughter. They headed over without pausing for thought and in no time at all the four of us were together in a fierce embrace. Jen would go back with my parents that night and spend a few weeks at home. In the meantime, the college arranged for her to move to a new room away from the main campus. Although she was sad to leave the friends she'd made there, she was beyond relieved to say goodbye to those four walls. Besides, in the months that followed, those friends would rally round her admirably.

My parents paid a visit to Sean and his family a few days later. I pleaded with them to let me go with them but they wouldn't even consider it. I'll never know exactly what was said but, to my knowledge, Jen never saw Sean again. My mother told me once that he was pitiful in his remorse that day. He admitted what he'd done with the condom and fell to pieces as he confessed. Weeping and begging to be allowed to see Jen. Professing his undying love for her and apologising over and over again. I've always found this difficult. I'd rather he denied any wrongdoing or claimed Jen was crazy or something. I'm unsure why. It didn't make me hate him any less, of course. In my darkest moments, I sometimes think it's because a whisper of that same pathetic weakness may lie within me. The capacity to be consumed by my own insecurities. To lose grip. To give in to a need for absolute love that is so unpalatable and repulsive as to make me shudder when I think of it.

It's impossible to know the extent to which the episode shaped my sister's life. She is the strongest person I know and so I'd love to think that she was able to move past it. But that may be naïve, or even selfish. Apart from in those first few weeks, it isn't something she speaks about but neither do I think she's buried it. It's always there, some-where. But it doesn't define her. She told me once, in the weeks that followed, that she didn't blame Sean for anything. He never forced himself on her or raised his hand to her. He was simply a broken little boy who couldn't cope with the world. Of the two of them, looking back, he was the more scared. Not for the first time, or the last, that conversation left me in total admiration of my sister. We can all fall foul of other people in this life, but my sister is nobody's victim.

≡

A thick silence hung in the air that even the racing wind could not penetrate.

'Did you hear me?'

I didn't answer. I couldn't. It was as though I'd been shot in the stomach and my body was in shock. The pain was spreading and the wound would kill me. I just couldn't feel it yet.

'Mate. Say something. Please.'

'What do you mean, you're dying?'

'I've been ... I've got Parkinson's.'

This snapped me out of my catatonic state. 'Don't be stupid. You can't have.'

'Mate...'

'Parkinson's is what old people get. That shaking thing, right?'

'Yeah. But you can get it young as well. It's not as common but there are loads of...'

'Is this a piss-take? Because it's not funny.'

'I wish it was, mate. But, look, it is what it is. There are ... I mean, people live long lives with it. Look, I didn't mean to be so ... I could live decades, it's just gonna be ... different.'

'Wait. So, are you dying or not?'

'Mate...'

'Answer.' I knew I was behaving appallingly. With every word that left my mouth I knew it. But I was angry, inexplicably angry. 'Answer!'

'I may be. But I might not ... I mean, it's ... I'll deteriorate.'

'This is bullshit.'

I would never forgive myself for what happened then. I stormed off. Like a selfish child. I left my friend standing on a muddy coastal path in the wind and rain. I ran away. Then I realised I had nowhere to go.

Rolly called to me. 'Mate, please!'

I stopped and pathetically walked back towards him. It was during those few steps that the numbness hit me for the first time. A poisonous protective liquid blanket coursing through my veins and flooding my insides. I stood to face him.

'I'm sorry. It's just. You know.'

'Of course, I'm sorry for just dumping it on you. I just … I wanted you to know. It's only you and Tabs that … and my folks, of course.'

'Right.' I couldn't look him in the eye. I couldn't feel the weight of this thing. This moment that would change everything forever.

'Mate, I'm really … I'm scared mate.'

I looked up at him to see his eyes fill with tears. I hugged him then and he wept on my shoulder. But I wasn't there. Not really. For the rest of that day I grew progressively colder. As we went through the motions of cleaning the cottages and packing up the car, I faked it. Rolly and Tabs spoke at me about the wedding and the illness, the light and the dark. I congratulated and commiserated. I nodded and hugged, smiled and looked sad. I don't know if Tabs realised right away what was happening. What I was doing. But Rolly did. He knew me better than I knew myself. He knew I had this in me. This inability. This lacking. I only spoke when spoken to. I was on autopilot.

Once the day was over and we were home I said good-night to them both. He held me tightly and tried to convey a million things in that embrace. I turned away from my friend, went into my room and shut the door. The next morning, I left a scribbled note advising that I was visiting my parents for a few weeks and would see them soon. I ran away. At first, I didn't tell my parents what had happened. They knew, of course, that something was wrong and kept asking me until, on the second day, Rolly called. I was at the pub at the time, drinking myself into a stupor for the first of many nights in a row. When I drunkenly stumbled through the front door, my parents were waiting for me. They confronted me about it all but I was gone. Drunk and useless. Wretched.

Over the next few weeks they tried many times to get through to me. To intervene and pull me from my well of self-pity. Looking back, it was only their efforts that prevented me from losing all grip on reality. I drank too much and wallowed in a selfishness so ugly as to almost be unthinkable. But they kept me together. Gave me structure and, crucially, time. Time I needed but didn't deserve. They slowly chipped away at me until I began, step by step, to face the truth. They gave me endless chores that peaked with a demand to drive my grandfather to Scotland and back. They instinctively knew, I think, that time with him would do me a world of good. And they were right. A few days later I dragged myself back to London to face my friend.

It was awful. I felt so utterly terrible and ashamed. He of course forgave me, as did Tabs. It was far more than I deserved. It hadn't been a sudden awakening for me. The news and the way forward hadn't broken through the numbness and hit me around the face. It had been a gradual, painful thing. But I was there now and determined to make things up to my friend. I'd let him down but I was resolute that I would never do so again. We spent that night planning the wedding and it was as though I had never done this terrible thing. As though the last few weeks hadn't happened at all.

My head still wasn't right and I continued to spend too many nights down the pub drinking alone over the next week or two. Then, on the night that I met a grey-haired and pale-skinned boy named Leon, life finally seemed to make some sort of sense again. I quickly went from one extreme to the other as I, somewhat naively, vowed to go through Rolly's experience of Parkinson's with him. I researched and studied the condition and bored both him and Tabs to death with endless facts and figures. Together we quickly came to understand that it wouldn't be the death sentence Rolly had thought it to be. The condition itself was unlikely to shorten his life expectancy on its own … but in its more advanced stages, it would leave my friend vulnerable to infections that could rob the world of this brilliant and beautiful young man. We also learnt that the rate at which it progresses varies massively from person to person and that there was a good chance that it could be years before Rolly even felt any significant impact on his day-to-day life. Suddenly the future and all the promise of a new millennium sprawled out before us once again.

As it turned out, Rolly's symptoms did progress at pace over the next couple of years. By the wedding – a joyous and life-affirming celebration of love and friendship – he was already noticeably slower in both his movement and speech. The tremors quickly became more impactful as well. He would get frustrated with himself, particularly if he started shaking during a meeting at work.

'Those bastards all thought I was nervous. That's what really gets me, you know?'

But in many ways his life continued as normal. In some ways even better than normal. His perspective altered in the face of his condition. His appreciation of beauty, of his wife, his friends, his family, all seemed to heighten and intensify. He accepted Parkinson's into his life and acknowledged its impact. But at no stage did he allow it to shape him. It was in the back of the car and, from time to time, would kick out at the seat in front and whine relentlessly. But Rolly was in the driving seat, always. This was his journey.

Something is different. The light beyond my closed eyes is moving. Breathing. A warm odorous breath. A drop of something wet. I open my eyes and there you are. Your face staring down into mine. Strands of saliva drooling and dropping onto my skin. Those weeping eyes, piercing through the hopelessness of daybreak. That torn ear with its dried crusting of blood. Am I dreaming? A low whimper. I smile. A broad and full smile of purest happiness.

'Hello you.'

Your tail wags at the sound of my cracked voice and your back end gives an involuntary dance of delight. I reach into my pocket and pull out a corner of stale pastry that I wrapped in tissue. Saving it for this moment. You devour it and the dance becomes more urgent and excited.

'Come here, you.'

You climb under the blanket. I wrap you in it. I protect you from the world. Together we are warm and safe. You fidget but then calm. You lay your head against mine and we sleep.

I have torn this city asunder. You are here. I have scorched the boundaries of this broken Babylon. I have scaled its sullied heights and plumbed its lonely depths. You are here. You found me. And when we awake it will ... at last ... be tomorrow.

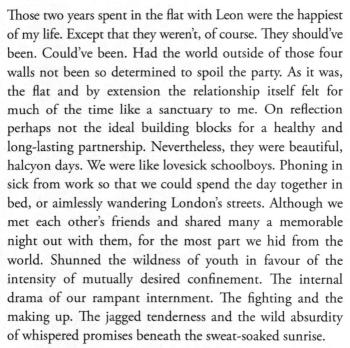

Those two years spent in the flat with Leon were the happiest of my life. Except that they weren't, of course. They should've been. Could've been. Had the world outside of those four walls not been so determined to spoil the party. As it was, the flat and by extension the relationship itself felt for much of the time like a sanctuary to me. On reflection perhaps not the ideal building blocks for a healthy and long-lasting partnership. Nevertheless, they were beautiful, halcyon days. We were like lovesick schoolboys. Phoning in sick from work so that we could spend the day together in bed, or aimlessly wandering London's streets. Although we met each other's friends and shared many a memorable night out with them, for the most part we hid from the world. Shunned the wildness of youth in favour of the intensity of mutually desired confinement. The internal drama of our rampant internment. The fighting and the making up. The jagged tenderness and the wild absurdity of whispered promises beneath the sweat-soaked sunrise.

For days, even weeks at a time, the flat was our entire world. With its frayed lime-green sofa, propped up on one corner by our spare copy of Bret Easton Ellis' *Glamorama* and a Gideon Bible, stolen by way of a defiant souvenir of our first night together in a hotel. Roughly plastered white walls covered in posters and art prints. Klimt beside Bowie. The Chemical Brothers next to Hopper's *Office in a Small City*. The battered turntable that lay on the floor and sound-tracked our every moment. The kitchenette with its chipped and worn faux-marble surfaces and banana-yellow walls. The never-made bed that bottled our combined perfume within its creases and folds. Unique and intoxicating. The sash window that looked out over the street beneath. Our street. Our own slice of London. We'd lean from it and smoke, laugh and watch the lives unfolding below us. None of them aware of the secret world above with only two inhabitants. Every last inch of that place is burned into my consciousness forever.

But there's only so much hiding I could do. The subplot to our vibrant and clichéd romantic drama was always creeping in the darkened corners. Writhing around in our peripheral vision and threatening to engulf the main narrative. And it was all mine. The relationship began under the shadow of my best friend's bombshell. From day one Leon assumed the role of carer. He was a sympathetic shoulder to cry on even before he was a lover. He guided me through those first few weeks after apologising to Rolly. Picked me up when I fell and whispered words of encouragement in my many moments of self-doubt. When the naked flame of new-found passion should have been burning at its brightest, he found himself looking after an emotional wreck of a boy he'd only just met.

And just when it seemed our love might find freedom and the space to spread its wings, Jen's news. News that crushed me all over again. Leon was second place in a field of one. My entire being was filled with a complex storm of emotions, all focusing on my sister. Yet still, he was there for me. Unquestioningly and unceasingly. When some dissenting voice from within must surely have been whispering to him to get out of this. Away from this toxic runt of the litter, doomed to lurch from one crisis to the next. Always in the throes of some desperate disaster. But he stayed. And somehow, we found room to blossom.

He got on well with all my family and friends, although I perhaps detected a quiet coldness between him and Rolly even from the outset. I, too, seemed to be accepted by his loved ones. Yet, neither of us ever truly integrated ourselves into each other's inner circle. Our relationship was always somehow separate. Set apart from friends and the world in general. But I don't want to overstate this, to retrospectively rewrite our time together in light of what I now know. There were many wonderful and noticeably ordinary shared experiences beyond the confines of our first-floor sanctuary. He was by my side at Rolly's wedding. Practising my best man's speech with me and beaming at me when I'd beaten the nerves and successfully delivered it. A standing ovation of one. I organised a giant surprise birthday party for him that involved bringing together his friends and family from throughout his lifetime. A lavish get-together in the basement of our favourite pub, where blown-up photographs of him adorned the wall space, charting his life from childhood to present day. I hired a local band that we both loved to play long into the night and sing Happy Birthday to him as the crowd joined in and his mother and I presented him with a ludicrously oversized three-tier cake.

We were, I believe, in many ways, genuinely happy throughout those first two years. Then, as the relationship matured, we began to speak about the next phase. I'd had enough of London and yearned for the West Country. Leon was surprisingly open to the idea of leaving the capital, considering he'd always been vocal about his love of the city. In the end we decided to head for Bristol and our first real home together. We bought a fixer upper in Brislington, an hour or so's walk from the city centre. A tumbledown 1930s terrace in need of more work than we could ever possibly afford. But it was ours. It was a wildly exciting time for both of us. A new and hopelessly grown-up chapter. One we hoped would be as exciting but less intense than our journey thus far. My parents rallied with offers to help with decorating and gifts of old furniture and white goods. It felt gloriously tangible. Like real life had arrived at last in all its fabulous mundanity.

Then, when it became clear what was happening to my grandfather, everything changed again. Our relationship would be put to the test once more. With the benefit of hindsight, I can see that, all things considered, this was a test it never really passed.

✕

'Pleasure to finally meet you. My name is Dr Alexander Shardlow. Call me Alex.'

'Alex, is he okay?'

'Yes, he's fine. Or he will be. He was badly beaten up as you know and then went through a period of time when he couldn't or wouldn't communicate with us. It's–'

'What, you mean he was ... brain damaged or something?'

'No, no, nothing like that. Initially we assumed perhaps a pre-existing condition but, well.'

'Well?'

'For whatever reason, he just didn't want to speak. He was completely silent and wouldn't even make eye contact. To be honest, I was hoping you might be able to provide the explanation for this behaviour. The brain is a funny thing of course, could simply be psychological trauma from the attack, but ... well, I'm the one who's spent most time with him and my belief is that this unwillingness to communicate pre-dates the attack. But, as I say, I'm hoping you may be able to tell me more–'

'How did you get him to speak?'

'The dog.'

'What?'

'Ah, I see you don't know the dog. Yes, its condition certainly suggests it's a stray.'

'What dog?'

'I don't really know, except that when the paramedics arrived, there was a dog clinging to him for dear life. It was just as badly beaten as he was. By all accounts it was a devil of a thing to convince the creature to let go of him. Anyway, he responded to talk of the animal. Wanted to know how it was and when he could see it. This means nothing to you at all?'

'No.'

'And this silence, this detachment. You know about that?'

'Yes. Yes, I think I do know about that.'

'I'd be very grateful if you could—'

'I'm sorry, Alex. Right now, I just really want to see my brother. Can you take me to him, please?'

'Yes, of course, Miss…'

'Jen, call me Jen.'

'Follow me, Jen.'

≡

It began, as I'd guess it usually does, with small things. Excusable things. Things that allowed you to pretend that there was no cause for concern. A kettle in the fridge. Not remembering how to work the TV controller. Then it grew, slowly at first, into something more troubling. Soap opera clichés that felt unreal. He'd forget the way home from the shops. He began to get our names mixed up or would momentarily forget them altogether. On one occasion at the dinner table, he thought Jen was my mother. We watched as he looked at us all and realised that that couldn't be the case. Confusion spread across his features. He tried to laugh it off and we let him. Although my parents were already talking about it to each other and beginning to accept the reality of it, none of us wanted it to be true.

It escalated quickly then and soon we were all forced to stare it in the face. It was undeniable. In what seemed like the blink of an eye, my grandfather had turned from a jovial, independent, larger than life character into a scared, confused and vulnerable old man. It was heart-breaking. I remember feeling a desperate desire to fix things. Falling into the trap of believing that I could somehow talk him out of it. The decision to put him in a care home ultimately fell to my mother, although she discussed it with all of us first on a night that ranked among the worst of all our lives. Once he was in the home, the rate of his decline was astonishing. For the rest of her own life, my mother would doubt her decision. Suggesting that, perhaps, he would have been okay for a little longer if she'd have just held off putting him in the home. I hope though, that somewhere deep down, she knew that wasn't true.

Naturally, we visited him every day. Sometimes all of us, other times just one or two of us. On one occasion, towards the end, I went alone. By this point, on the surface, the man was unrecognisable. A shadow of his former self. He sat hunched and afraid in his bed, the rotund, rosy cheeks replaced by a pale gaunt man I no longer knew.

'Hello, Grandpa.'

He looked at me, unknowing, and offered a cautious smile. 'Have you seen my wife?'

'No, not today, Grandpa.'

'Oh. I'm sure she'll be along shortly. She's pregnant, you know?'

'Oh?'

'A girl. They won't tell me but I know it's a girl. That nurse there, she knows as well … I can see she does.'

I settled into the chair beside his bed and held his frail hand. Although a part of me had got used to this, it never stopped being painful. I wanted to scream. To beg the world to make this stop, reverse it somehow. I could not, would not accept that I was losing him. Then after a few moments of silence, he squeezed my hand. I looked at him and in his pale eyes I saw my grandfather.

'Hello, my boy, when did you get here?'

Tears began to roll down my cheeks then. 'Hello, Grandpa.'

'Did I ever tell you about the time old Trigger saved me from the billy goat?'

'No, Grandpa, you never did.'

'Well now, let me see. I was only a nipper, can't have been more than ten, I reckon. I was helping my neighbours clean out their goats, in exchange for a bit of pocket money. He went away somewhere ... the neighbour, I forget his name. Then I was on my own in this pen with the goats, you see? Shovelling the muck and hay I was. Then this bloody billy goat charged at me. I'd never trusted that thing with its beady eyes. That's the problem though, he could tell I was scared of him. Never let an animal know you're scared of it, my boy. Anyway, he had these great horns and he was ramming me up against the fence. He could've killed me with those things, make no mistake. As it was, I was covered in bruises for weeks.

'Anyway, I was screaming merry hell. Bawling my eyes out and crying for someone to help. Nobody heard me. It felt like it went on for hours but I expect it was only a minute or two. Then I heard a bark. I turned and Trigger was bounding over. Charging he was. He crawled under the fence and didn't hesitate, went straight for the billy goat. Trigger was the biggest softy you'd ever meet. And a right old scaredy cat too. Yet, at that moment, he was a wild beast. His fur was sticking up and his teeth were snarling. He ripped the billy goat's neck open right in front of me. That goat was bigger than him, mind. But he didn't know what hit him. Trigger was in a rage it seemed. I just sat there sobbing quietly watching it all.

'Then he finished ... Trigger, I mean. He walked to me and sat himself down in front of me, with his back to me, panting and staring straight at the other goats. He was protecting me. None of them dared move. Soon the neighbour came back and at first he were ready to give Trigger a kicking but I shouted at him what had just happened. When my parents found out, well ... Old Trigger had a steak for his tea that night.

'I never forgot it. It was love, you see? Love of family. There is none stronger. I was Trigger's family and it didn't matter if he was normally a coward or a softy. When he saw I was in danger, he just did what he had to do. Family, my boy. You understand? It's not about names or blood or anything else like that. It's about being a pack. The love between a family is like nothing else on this earth. It will raise you up. And that's how I love you, my boy. And your mother and your sister … and your father for that matter. Just like it was with my mother and father … and old Trigger. You're part of something. You're the same. You understand me?'

'Yes, Grandpa. I understand you.'

I understood him more than he would ever know. That story, which he'd told us so many times. A story about the love of family over anything else. A story he told over and over again to make the point that family was the most important thing in the world. He didn't miss a beat. It was, word for word, as it had always been. So imperative and engrained in him was the love he had for his family that even through the thick nightmarish fog of dementia, he remembered every last detail of it. That was the last conversation I ever had with my grandfather. Or rather, the last one that either of us understood. The last one where he was really there.

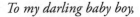

To my darling baby boy,

Happy birthday! Your dad and I can't wait to see you tomorrow, although we're both sure that there must be some sort of mistake. How can you possibly be thirty years old?! It seems like only yesterday that they put that little messy bundle of loveliness in my arms and everything changed forever. I wanted to write something down for you on this special occasion because ... well, because you're just like your father and you won't let me say any of it to your face without getting all fidgety and uncomfortable. How that happened I'll never know. Of all the things you could have got from your dad, you chose emotional embarrassment. Honestly, the two of you will turn red at the slightest thing. What a pair. Then there's your sister standing on stage in front of hundreds of people without a care in the world. Where she got that from, I've no idea. Anyway, I've wandered off the point.

I suppose I just wanted you to know how much you mean to us. Not just your dad and me but Jen and Grandpa as well. I know things aren't easy with your grandfather at the moment, my love, and I know how much you're struggling with it. A mother always knows. You've always been a sensitive soul. That, you did get off your mother, I'm afraid. But I know how much he loves you and how proud he is of you. You've always been his favourite. He loves us all to the ends of the earth of course, but he's always been totally smitten with his special little boy. He'd want you to enjoy your special day, my love.

He'd hate to think that you spent it worrying about him. I remember when he first laid eyes on you. I watched him melt right in front of me. But then, he wasn't alone in that. You were such a pretty little thing. Everyone turned to putty the first time they saw you.

It wasn't all fun and games, mind you. You were a little bugger sometimes. For a start, you didn't want to come out! Nearly three weeks late! I was fit to burst. I remember those three weeks like they were yesterday. Your father had read something in the papers about how you could do things to help the baby along. You should've seen him. He'd press his face to my belly and chat away to you for hours on end. Trying to talk you out! 'Now come on then, my lovely, let's have no more of this hiding, we're all waiting to meet you, you know.'

He'd sing and play records to you. I must've sat through every album that blasted Tom Jones ever made. He always did have a terrible music taste, your dad. I'd have killed for a bit of Bowie but no. 'Delilah' and 'What's New Pussycat'. If I'd had to sit through the Green, Green Grass of bloody Home one more time, I'd have pulled you out of there myself just for some peace and quiet. Then there was the food. Hot food, he'd read, helped things along. Guaranteed, he'd confidently declare. There were no curry houses near us in those days, of course. So, your father bought a great big jar of chilli powder and coated everything we ate in it. I couldn't taste anything at all for the first six months after you were born. My taste buds had been burned clean off. I swear it's why you love your spicy food so much. He was a sweetie though. He waited on me hand and foot. I didn't get any of the crazy cravings you hear about. Didn't with Jen either. But one night I pretended I had a craving for mushy peas covered in Bovril, just to see what he'd do about it. He drove for miles to find a chip shop still open

*and an all-night garage that would sell him some Bovril. I
had the best night's sleep I'd had in ages. No one fussing round
me. When I woke up, there he was, pleased as punch with
himself, holding up a bowl of stone-cold mushy peas covered in
Bovril like it was a trophy. It turned my stomach.*

*Then one afternoon it all started happening. We rushed to
the hospital. Well, I say that ... your father insisted we pick up
your grandfather on the way! 'I'll never hear the end of it if he
misses it.'*

*The birth was ... well, like I said, you were a little bugger
sometimes. But then there you were, lying in my arms, helpless
and small. You were a boy (but you know that, of course, ha!).
We didn't know, you see? If you'd been a girl, we'd have called
you Tammy! Did I ever tell you that? Well, it was the seventies!
Lucky escape, eh? It makes me laugh when I think about it
now. It was love at first sight. You were the most beautiful
thing I'd ever seen. I promised you then that I'd love you until
the day I died. That while I walked this earth nobody would
ever dare harm you. My darling baby boy.*

*And that promise stands. You and your sister are the best things
that ever happened to us. I'm proud of you every single day.
When I see the man you've become, I know I must have done
something right. A kind man who loves his family and friends.
Rocks to each other, you and that Rolly are. And to your sister.
And a brave man. It can't have been easy to come out of the
closet (why is it the closet? Honestly, why do we have to use
American words all the time nowadays? What's wrong with a
wardrobe, that's what I'd like to know?) but you did it and I'm
proud of you, son. And Leon's lovely. He's lucky to have you
and I hope he never forgets that, or he'll have me to answer to!*

*So, whatever life may bring you, remember this: You're my boy.
My soldier. Your family adores you, loves you unconditionally*

for all of time. And did I mention that we're all proud of you? Ha, I might have! Have a wonderful, amazing birthday my beautiful bouncing baby boy. You deserve it.

I love you always,
Mum xxx

≡

Dad: SON ITS YOUR DAD
My Number: Hi Dad, you OK?
Dad: YES IM TEXTING YOU ON MY NEW PHONE
My Number: Oooh fancy, when did you get that?
Dad: TODAY ITS NOKIA
My Number: Oh, right. Nice?
Dad: YES IT WAS THE BIGGEST IN THE SHOP
My Number: Ah OK. Is that good?
Dad: YES MAN SAID BEST ONE
My Number: Is it loud where you are?
Dad: ?
My Number: Don't worry. You pleased with it then?
Dad: YES YOUR MUM SAYS HI
My Number: Hi Mum!
Dad: WERE WATCHING NEW MISS MARPLE
My Number: Any good?
Dad: NO RUBBISH YOUR MUM SAYS NOT LIKE BOOK
My Number: Ah OK, never mind
Dad: BYE FOR NOW LOVE DAD
My Number: Bye then, Dad x

***

Dad: SON ITS YOUR DAD
My Number: Hi Dad, you OK?
Dad: YES IS THIS YOUR NUMBER
My Number: Eh?

Dad: I DELETED MY NUMBERS BY MISTAKE
My Number: Oh dear
Dad: IS THIS YOUR NUMBER
My Number: Well, yeah … of course
Dad: OK BYE SON
My Number: Bye Dad x

***

Dad: HI SON ITS YOUR DAD
My Number: Hi Dad, you OK?
Dad: CANT SLEEP
My Number: Me neither
Dad: WORRIED ABOUT YOUR GRANDPA
My Number: Me too
Dad: SAW HIM TODAY HE DIDN'T KNOW ME
My Number: It's hard. He thought I was you the other day
Dad: REALLY UPSET YOUR MUM
My Number: I know, how is she bearing up in general?
Dad: OK SHES A STRONG ONE
My Number: That's for sure
Dad: YOU KNOW YOU CAN TALK TO ME ANYTIME IF YOU NEED
My Number: Of course, I know Dad. Thanks x
Dad: TELLY RUBBISH LATE AT NIGHT
My Number: Yeah, I'm just listening to my headphones
Dad: TOM JONES?
My Number: Ha!
Dad: ITS NOT UNUSUAL
My Number: Very good!
Dad: OK BYE SON LOVE YOU
My Number: Bye then Dad, love you too x

***

My Number: Hi Dad, you awake?

Dad: HI SON ITS YOUR DAD

My Number: Can't sleep?

Dad: NO YOU EITHER

My Number: No

Dad: YOU SEE GRANDPA TODAY

My Number: Yes, he didn't know I was there though

Dad: ITS HARD SON YOU KNOW HE LOVES YOU THOUGH
HES COMFORTABLE AND THEYRE TAKING GOOD
CARE OF HIM IN THERE

My Number: I know. I just can't bear to think of life when
he's gone

Dad: I KNOW

My Number: It makes me think of you and Mum and
Jen. I can't stop thinking about it

Dad: WHAT YOU MEAN

My Number: How it would be if you weren't here anymore

Dad: WERE GOING NOWHERE SON

My Number: I know

Dad: I PROMISE

My Number: I know, thanks Dad. I'm just being silly

Dad: NOT SILLY IM AWAKE THINKING ABOUT HOW SAD
YOUR MUM WILL BE

My Number: She's a strong one

Dad: THATS FOR SURE

My Number: We'll all be there for her, like she's always
there for us

Dad: GOOD BOY I KNOW WE STICK TOGETHER

My Number: What you watching?

Dad: MISS MARPLE

My Number: At 3am?

Dad: RECORDED

My Number: I thought it was rubbish?

Dad: NO ITS BRILLIANT YOU CANT PLEASE YOUR MUM
      SHE LOVES THE BOOKS WHAT YOU WATCHING

My Number: Listening to records

Dad: AT 3AM GLAD IM NOT YOUR NEIGHBOUR

My Number: Headphones

Dad: NEVER HEARD OF THEM ARE THEY NEW BAND

My Number: Ha! Very good!

Dad: YOU OK

My Number: Yeah, you?

Dad: BETTER NOW IVE SPOKEN TO YOU

My Number: Me too

Dad: LOVE YOU SON NIGHT NIGHT X

My Number: Love you Dad, night night x

■

These days are new. Something other. In-between. This is not the void. Not as it has been. But neither have I left it. Our escape is pending. I need these times to … ready myself. To read tomorrow's pathways. To map them out. I follow you through this wasteland and as I do, I see things that were not there in the night. In the darkness. Shoots of life. Flecks of colour. Suggestions of … I cannot tell. You are in charge. You lead us through the no-man's land. We stop outside a supermarket and I tell you to wait for me. I think I've been to this place before but cannot be sure when. I buy dog food. Turkey and chicken in jelly. As I watch you eat it, I feel a sense of completeness that almost overcomes me. Your tail wags and you pause every few seconds to look up at me. As if to reiterate your gratitude or else to check that I'm still there. When you're finished, I pour water from a plastic bottle on to the pavement so that you can lap at it as it cascades downward.

As we walk on, I take a deep, deliberate breath. Behind the fumes and scent of decay, I can smell something else. Not a freshness exactly. But an openness. A smell of space. We walk through a park and stop by a flower bed. The flowers are pink and yellow and orange. They are exhaust-blackened at the very edges but the colours are vibrant. They reach us. We see them. We walk into the public lavatories and I wash my face and hands in the sink. I can feel the water as it soaks my skin. There are phone numbers scribbled on the walls asking for sexual acts but there are other things written there as well. A joke: 'Don't beam me up, Scotty, I'm taking a shiiiiii…' This makes me smile and when I look down at you, my smile widens.

We spend the day wandering like this. Together, stronger. Past the flickering lights and faceless gleaming shopfronts. Past smiling faces on advertising boards as they fade in and out, in and out. Past the mirrored office buildings and derelict factories. Past overflowing bins and steamy-windowed cafes. Along pavements and footpaths as traffic endlessly grinds and shimmers. I'm conscious of all this but I'm not lost in it. It is the background to the journey but it is not the journey. We are the journey. I watch you move, prance and scratch. You fill the empty world. Give it back its beauty.

'I'm going to call you Marmite.'

You wag your tail.

'But not because of your colour.'

You turn your head to one side.

'Because I love you even though you smell bad.'

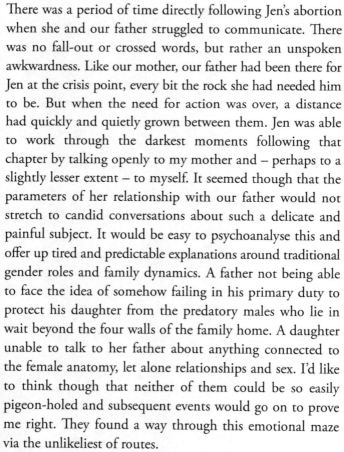

There was a period of time directly following Jen's abortion when she and our father struggled to communicate. There was no fall-out or crossed words, but rather an unspoken awkwardness. Like our mother, our father had been there for Jen at the crisis point, every bit the rock she had needed him to be. But when the need for action was over, a distance had quickly and quietly grown between them. Jen was able to work through the darkest moments following that chapter by talking openly to my mother and – perhaps to a slightly lesser extent – to myself. It seemed though that the parameters of her relationship with our father would not stretch to candid conversations about such a delicate and painful subject. It would be easy to psychoanalyse this and offer up tired and predictable explanations around traditional gender roles and family dynamics. A father not being able to face the idea of somehow failing in his primary duty to protect his daughter from the predatory males who lie in wait beyond the four walls of the family home. A daughter unable to talk to her father about anything connected to the female anatomy, let alone relationships and sex. I'd like to think though that neither of them could be so easily pigeon-holed and subsequent events would go on to prove me right. They found a way through this emotional maze via the unlikeliest of routes.

The four of us were sprawled lazily across the sofas in the family homestead one Sunday afternoon, all set to spend the next few hours sleeping off a gargantuan roast dinner.

As I dozed in front of the TV and Murray Walker's voice began to fade from consciousness, I was vaguely aware of my father saying something to Jen and the two of them leaving the room. The next thing I remember is being gently shaken awake by my mother.

'Come on, you've got to see this.'

She led me, bleary-eyed, to the kitchen window and gestured for me to look out into the back garden. There stood Jen and my father side by side ... digging.

'They've been out there nearly two hours.'

My father's vegetable patches consumed the vast majority of the back garden by this point. A colourful, regimented landscape of runner beans, courgettes and cauliflowers. Spinach, chard, lettuce leaves and vibrant red tomatoes. My mother and I stood and watched through the window as the two of them dug and watered, shovelled and composted.

They were talking the whole while, we assumed primarily about the job at hand. To the best of my knowledge, Jen had never shown the slightest interest in any aspect of gardening or growing before. Yet she looked utterly at home in her new environment, in her element even. After another twenty minutes or so, the two of them became engrossed in conversation, downed tools and stopped what they were doing. My father placed a gentle hand on Jen's shoulder and they were soon locked in a loving embrace. Through the pane of glass, we could see the tears rolling down both their faces and realised we were now eavesdropping on a very personal moment.

'Come on,' my mother said, 'let's go and see what Murray's up to.'

And so began the life of Jen the gardener. Over the next few years, she and my father would cement a bond that would never be broken. There can be little doubt that it began simply as a way for my father to extract Jen from the family setting, wherein he found it impossible to express the things he needed to say to his beloved daughter. A way of giving both of them the time and space they needed to be able to open up to one another. But then it grew (pardon the pun) into something different. Not only did Jen and our father become confidantes and discover a new level of closeness and understanding of one another, but Jen also found a genuine passion for all things green.

She'd spend many of her precious weekends helping my father tend to the garden while her friends were out enjoying the bars and clubs of London's nightlife. Eventually – after being on the waiting list for some eighteen months – she got a plot at a coveted allotment a few miles from her rented flat in the capital. Whenever my parents visited us, father and daughter would disappear for hours on end so that Jen could proudly show off her latest successes and my father could offer sage advice (that one was deliberate) and share the wisdom of his many years of experience.

Having spent so much of my early years by my father's side as I accompanied him to endless rallycross events, I understood the pleasure Jen felt from this new bond. The richness and depth of happiness that came from having his full and undivided attention. As I witnessed them both enjoying their shared interest as this new facet of their relationship bloomed (again, sorry), it sent a rush of warmth through me. I know my mother felt the same way. Which isn't to say that we weren't both bored to the point of unconsciousness by their endless conversations about sprouts and slug management, of course. Many future family meals together would begin with my mother cautioning,

'Now, we'll have no talk of vegetables from you two while we're eating, okay?' She'd then flash me a knowing smile and I'd chip in with the well-rehearsed, 'Indeed, vegetables have no place at this dinner table.'

■

After the light, the dark. Creeping over the new things that we have found. Enfolding us. An endless irresistible shadow that hides from view the winding path leading us to home. The flickering light that finally surrenders to the encroaching blackness. But ... not quite. For even the dark night is something different now. It is full. The world is sleeping beneath this boundless cloak but it's still there. It is not emptied or altered. The breath of life is slow and hushed but the heart beats on. We are not in the empty space, you and I. No longer of it.

Yet, not everything beyond the numbness is an old friend with arms outstretched. It's fear that greets me now. What if I cannot get past this moment of salvation? The endless tomorrow, no more than a new form of purgatory. Where we roam, unburdened but still lost to all but each other. A limbo I've drawn you into with the whispered promise of a new dawn. The figures that float and burst beneath my eyelids are no longer the ghosts of layers lost. They are the screaming souls of those I've left behind but now must face. Their questions still unanswered. What if the same man lies in wait beyond the blankness? Weak and wretched and broken and impotent.

You sense my fear. Your weeping eyes see the truth of me but do not turn away. I shun the numbness and inhale the fear. I hold you close and we face the darkness together.

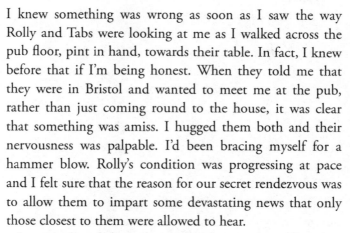

I knew something was wrong as soon as I saw the way Rolly and Tabs were looking at me as I walked across the pub floor, pint in hand, towards their table. In fact, I knew before that if I'm being honest. When they told me that they were in Bristol and wanted to meet me at the pub, rather than just coming round to the house, it was clear that something was amiss. I hugged them both and their nervousness was palpable. I'd been bracing myself for a hammer blow. Rolly's condition was progressing at pace and I felt sure that the reason for our secret rendezvous was to allow them to impart some devastating news that only those closest to them were allowed to hear.

I remember feeling a twinge of annoyance that they hadn't deemed Leon worthy of their confidence. He and Rolly had never quite clicked. They got on okay with one another on a surface level. Each of them was vocal in their regard of the other but there always seemed an indefinable something between them. Not quite mistrust, not quite dislike, but a definite sense of discomfort in each other's company. Still, Leon was to me as Tabs was to Rolly and the idea of leaving her out of such an undertaking, were the roles reversed, seemed so strange to me as to be absurd.

'So come on, guys, what's with the secret meeting place?'

They looked at each other then. I tried to read their eyes but couldn't. It didn't seem right though. Their nervousness was *wrong* somehow.

It was Rolly that spoke. In that slightly slowed down and

deliberate manner that I'd become used to over the recent months. 'Mate, this isn't going to be easy. To say or to hear.'

'Right … okay.'

'It's about Leon.'

As he said those words, an icy chill swept over me. All the quiet fear I'd been carrying around in my belly since I'd spoken to them on the phone fell away, to be replaced with something rigid. Something stony and stand-offish. Looking back, I wonder if I knew what was coming then. Whether I could suddenly see it on their faces or else somewhere deep down I'd already suspected it.

'Okay.'

'He was in London last weekend, right?'

'Yeah, he was visiting friends.'

'Right. So, I … that is, we…' He gestured to Tabs, who was biting her bottom lip and looking as though she'd like nothing more than to bolt for the door. '…we saw him.'

'Okay.'

'We were out at a club. It was Tabs' friends leaving do. Actually, it's that one we went to for your birthday that one time, run by Mr What's-his-face … from The Shamen.'

'The End?'

'Yeah, that's it, The End. That was a great night, wasn't it?'

'Rolly, spit it out, mate.'

'Right. Well, the thing is … he wasn't alone. You know?'

'He was with friends?'

'Right, but, the thing is. This guy … he wasn't a friend, mate. They were … well, to be honest, they were…'

'What were they, Rolly?'

'They were all over each other.' It was Tabs who cut in with this as she saw her husband struggling to deliver the unthinkable final blow.

188

'What?'

'I'm sorry, mate, I didn't want to … I'm, I'm sorry.'

I sat in silence with a dumb look of confusion sprawled across my face.

Tabs spoke then. Just to break the silence, I think. 'He's been so worried about telling you. He loves you, you know that, right? We both do and we're so, so sorry.'

And then, tiresomely and predictably, I replied. 'No, look, you've just read the situation wrong is all. Leon's very, he's very tactile with his friends. It may have looked … but it will just have been … honestly, it's nothing like that.'

They looked at each other and this time I could read their expressions all too clearly and found that I had to fight back a rush of anger. Their faces were etched with a knowing pity.

'Look, mate. That's not what it was, they were–'

'Rolly!' I said his name too loudly, too angrily and then tried to turn it into something jovial. As though I found my friends' misunderstanding amusing. 'Guys, seriously, you've got it wrong. That's not Leon. He'd just tell me if he'd met … I mean, it's ridiculous. I know you mean well, guys, but, I mean, it's ridiculous.'

'They were kissing, their hands were all over each other. They left together. Alone, together.' Tabs delivered this killer blow quickly and concisely, before I could cut in.

'You guys have never liked him, right? I know it and he knows it too. I get it, but this isn't cool.'

'For Christ's sake, do you really think we'd…'

I got up to leave but as I did, Tabs grabbed my wrist. 'No! You don't walk out on him again.'

Rolly touched her arm and calmly and quietly said, 'Tabs, it's okay.'

'No. It isn't. It isn't okay.' She turned to face me again.

'You sit down and you deal with this. You don't put my husband through losing you again just because he was a good enough friend to tell you the ugly truth you needed to hear. You do not do that!'

I tried to stop the anger of denial from rising up in me at that moment. I really did. On some level her words did penetrate my thick skull. On some level I knew that she was *of course* right. But I couldn't do it. Fight or flight? I flew, as I always had.

'Fuck you.'

I spat the words and yanked my arm from her grasp. I turned and walked from the pub without looking back.

'Fuck you, too.' That was Rolly, not Tabs. Three angry, slurred words to end decades of friendship.

By the time I arrived home I should – by rights – have been a trembling wreck of remorse and fury. My only thought should have been what I did first: call my friends to beg for their forgiveness or steel myself to confront Leon. But that didn't happen. I was numb. I was calm and empty. I erased the day from existence. I erased my friends. I let the numbness fill the empty space.

They come for us in the night. As we lie entwined beneath that boundless cloak. Our breath slow and hushed as our hearts beat on. Dreaming of our new dawn.

We awake amid a rancid cloud of spit and laughter. I instinctively reach for you but you are baring your teeth and standing to face them. A fallen warrior angel lost in the fires of hell. Words spew from them then. Vile, gleeful, hate-filled. The first blow is to your ribcage. You howl with pain and I am awake then. I scream at them. They are the void. They swarm and I am lost again. I yell and shriek amid the kicks and punches. The numbness offers itself to me and the void door opens. You run at them, trying to put yourself between them and me. They kick and punch and their hatred shatters you. You cry and whimper and howl into the void.

And the sound of it kills me but then enables me to be born again. Born as rage and fury and light. I bite and rip and tear. I roar at the numbness and I see that it cowers in the face of this burning pain. I climb on top of your sobbing body and lock myself in place. Braced against the night. The void kicks and punches and screams. Its putrid deafening laughter is raining down on us in hissing, shrieking torrents. Darkness pouring over our bleeding broken form. But we are the light and you shine through me as I lay covering you. Shielding you from all the dark nights we have known. From the loneliness and the empty space. I know I must go through the door and give in to the numbness.

Through the pain I am resigned to it. But I will not let it take you. I will not give it your light. When you wake from this, it will be tomorrow.

Shouts through the night. Running footsteps and the void retreats. Still laughing and spitting at the light. As it pulls away from us and back into itself, a final hate-filled blow lands on the side of my head and I know I cannot keep the numbness at bay any longer. I fall then. Collapse into the blankness forever.

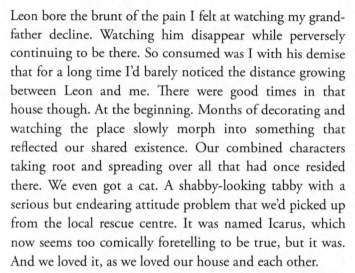

Leon bore the brunt of the pain I felt at watching my grand-father decline. Watching him disappear while perversely continuing to be there. So consumed was I with his demise that for a long time I'd barely noticed the distance growing between Leon and me. There were good times in that house though. At the beginning. Months of decorating and watching the place slowly morph into something that reflected our shared existence. Our combined characters taking root and spreading over all that had once resided there. We even got a cat. A shabby-looking tabby with a serious but endearing attitude problem that we'd picked up from the local rescue centre. It was named Icarus, which now seems too comically foretelling to be true, but it was. And we loved it, as we loved our house and each other.

But I had exhausted Leon's capacity to be the relationship's caregiver. To be met by abject misery at the end of each day slowly became more than he was willing to tolerate. At first, he simply became short-tempered. Snapping at me over small everyday things that previously wouldn't have mattered. His sympathy for me regarding the situation with my grandfather waned until it was no longer there at all. He simply didn't want to hear about it anymore. Then slowly he began to drift away from me. Imperceivably at first, working late at the office. An increasing number of weekends away with friends. Then I began to register, even through my strange and ugly pre-emptive grief, that I was alone more often than not. If I'm honest with myself, I struggled to care.

The oppressive sadness I felt about my grandfather was swiftly transforming into a more widespread form of depression. I could no longer look at myself in the mirror. I wasn't sleeping. Endless nights of deafening silence and high-speed stillness as my mind raced along, alone in the darkness. The days were blurred exercises in pretence. Awkward meetings with bosses, colleagues and friends where I hazily assured them that I was fine. The one thing on each day's to-do list being to make it through to the end. And then the nights. When suddenly the fuzziness cleared and I was in some manic, heightened state of awareness. The world rushed around my head ceaselessly. Fear and futility sparring for dominance in a bloody battle of attrition. The dirt-smeared claws of insomnia dug into my pallid skin during those endless nights and have never fully unclasped themselves from me.

There were attempts to make things work. To fix them. He surprised me one evening with Eurostar tickets to Paris. I beckoned every last drop of strength I had for that weekend, some oppressed part of me inherently understanding the importance of it. The last chance saloon. And there were moments. A wonderfully vulgar kiss beneath the Arc de Triomphe. Laughter as we reeled off increasingly laboured crepe jokes. Nothing beats a good chocolatey crepe at breakfast time. You get the idea. We slept together for the first time in months. And the last time ever. The lack of sex was in itself an undeniable sign of our pending demise. Leon's libido had always been insane. In the early days he was insatiable. No space private or public was off limits. From train toilets to country parks and office car parks. But that was before I became repulsive to him. There is very little in this world as unattractive as self-pity. It has a stench of its own that causes all about it to recoil. Yet, almost unbelievably, we lurched on like this. The months rolling into years until we'd been broken for longer than we were ever whole. Two strangers living separate lives under the same roof.

I should have confronted him after talking to Rolly. I should've believed my friend. But then, it was worse than that, of course. Because I did believe my friend. I just couldn't summon the strength or focus to face the truth so savagely sprawled out before me. So, I stayed silent as I continued to spiral. I ignored the truth and simply kept falling. Until the sky was no longer in sight. Until there was only the darkness of the endless frenzied night. Where my impotent vapid body lay motionless as my thrashing racing mind screamed at the closed door of the void.

✕

For the first few seconds, I can't remember where I am. Then the room slowly comes into focus. The off-white walls adorned with laminated posters instructing people to wash their hands or how to recognise a stroke victim. The cold shine of the light-blue plastic flooring and the rumble of voices from beyond the partition wall.

You were in my dream again last night. The only light in the endless darkness of my nightmares. I think together maybe we can do this. I wish I hadn't ... I mean, I burn to see her. But I ... how can she forgive me?

The door opens and a nurse walks in. The tall one with the birth mark on her neck. It's shaped like a billy goat. I don't like it; it makes me think she's going to attack me. I close my eyes and pretend to be asleep, just like always. She knows I'm not but doesn't care. Why would she? She checks things to the side of me and writes something on the clipboard at the end of my bed. When I hear the door close, I open my eyes again. I try and keep them open when there's nobody in the room. I see things when I close them. Even if I'm not asleep. Their faces mainly. Smiling or crying. Sometimes screaming or decaying.

Soon I'll come and get you and we can ... well, I don't know what we'll do. Or where we'll go. But whatever, and wherever, we'll be together. Alex told me you clung to me when the ambulance turned up and wouldn't let go. My protector. When I'm out of here, I'll protect you always. Forever. I'll never let you down as I let the others down. I promise.

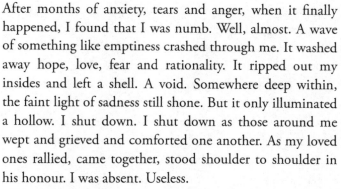

After months of anxiety, tears and anger, when it finally happened, I found that I was numb. Well, almost. A wave of something like emptiness crashed through me. It washed away hope, love, fear and rationality. It ripped out my insides and left a shell. A void. Somewhere deep within, the faint light of sadness still shone. But it only illuminated a hollow. I shut down. I shut down as those around me wept and grieved and comforted one another. As my loved ones rallied, came together, stood shoulder to shoulder in his honour. I was absent. Useless.

The crematorium was a vast red brick cube surrounded by a tarmacked car park. Unhidden and functional. Purpose built for the disposal of all that remains when the roaring flame of life has been extinguished. The empty vase. The residue. When love and dreams and soul and laughter are gone forever. Silence. Silence and the shadow of the chimneys above.

I stood with those who knew him. Those who loved him as I did and their serious, solemn-faced plus-ones. Leon bowed his head beside me in dignified respect but never a comforting hand was felt. No reassuring squeeze or sad soothing smile. My mother wept yet stood strong. The tears fell but her chin jutted in defiance of the truth. She met it head on, as her father would have wanted. My father stood by her side, his own eyes watery and blurred as he clasped my mother's hand in his. Jen linked her arm through his other and perhaps her other through mine. I'm unsure.

Rolly and Tabitha, whom my mother had invited, stood behind me somewhere. Maybe crying, maybe not. Maybe wanting to comfort their estranged friend and maybe not. I knew some of the other mourners. Others I recognised but could not place. Some I'd never seen, or had long since forgotten. Faces made uglier for the fact that he would never look upon them again. Withered by his absence.

People spoke, then stopped speaking. Words of kindness and words of pity. Poetry and prose. 'Stop the Clocks' and 'Death Be Not Proud'. The brilliant white walls, bright but respectfully plain, the neutral brown carpet that hid the dirt smeared by a million mourning footsteps as death marches on forever and ever, Amen. Cold, uncomfortable wooden benches, varnished to a sheen. A colourful bouquet slowly dying in one corner. A5 black-and-white print-outs displaying the order of business, the formality of death. A grainy picture of his face. Smiling. Forever. The woman conducting the service tilts her head in perfected sympathy for perhaps the second or third time today. Just another day in the office. Time is of the essence. We move on with appropriate swiftness. There are more who must mourn today. The right speaker plays as the left just crackles. Its need to be fixed or replaced will be on somebody's to-do list. His favourite song plays: 'I Love You Much Too Much' by the Andrews Sisters. Their distant tender voices ring out across the room, tinny and cracked, as he slowly disappears through the black curtains. Before the song finishes, we begin to file out, one row at a time. Heads down, no fuss. I have a brief urge to scream, to run through the curtains and grab the coffin. To pull it from its conveyer belt before the flames engulf it. Engulf him. But then it passes and the blankness floods the space once more.

I stayed like this for days. Unreachable and unhelpful. Mine was a selfish grief. I did not comfort those I loved, who missed him as desperately as I did. I did not smile and remember the good times. I did not do him that honour. I let him down.

Then, a week or so after the funeral, Jen and I walked from my parents' house to his. We were to begin the overdue task of sorting through his things. The house had stood empty for months by that point. My mother had been round to clean a few times when he first went into the home, but other than that, it had remained a lifeless space. Mourning him for longer than the rest of us. Unenviable decisions lay ahead. What to keep, what to discard. What value did each of his possessions hold to us? Jen turned the key in the grubby white PVC front door and we were inside. The silence hit us like a slap to the face. The dark emptiness of the house that had once been so warm and welcoming. The ash in the fireplace. The wall clock in the kitchen that ticked for no one. I moved through the space, staring but not seeing.

We began in the kitchen. My mother had removed all of the fresh produce and anything that could spoil, but there were still tinned goods and electrical devices. Cutlery that would never be used again. I opened a cupboard at random and immediately saw an unmistakable sight poking out from behind the jars of preserves and bottled condiments. I pulled out a bag of pink and white marshmallows and stared at it. I stood there staring down at it for five minutes. Maybe less, maybe more. And then it happened. Finally.

I began to cry and could not stop. I was soon curled up on the floor sobbing and heaving uncontrollably. From somewhere, Jen appeared and held me in her arms. She cried with me. I'm unsure if her tears were for him or for me. Tears of relief that I'd finally been able to do this. This thing that everyone else had done immediately upon hearing the news. This instinct of grief. This roar of pain so unnaturally missing in me over the last few weeks. I wept until there was nothing left and then I wept some more. My heart exploded with a sorrow that killed me and then allowed me to be reborn. The silence broke.

'You took your time,' whispered Jen as the sobs slowly began to subside. I clung to her with everything I had. 'It's okay ... it's okay. I've got you, bro, I've got you.'

We left that empty house, still so full of him, only to return a few days later. On that occasion my parents accompanied us and we met the ghosts within those four walls together. Among the tears I also smiled, even laughed, as Jen and I found rows of near-identical cardigans and white shirts in the ornate wardrobe that stood in his bedroom. I held in an overwhelming sadness as my mother found the key that unlocked the large drawer beneath it. I couldn't bring myself to look again at the contents that lay within, but I held my mother as she wept at the truth of it.

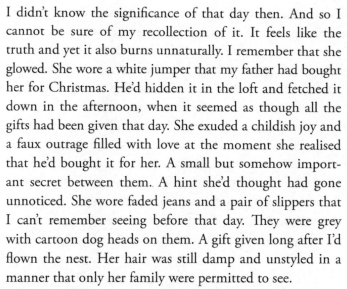

I didn't know the significance of that day then. And so I cannot be sure of my recollection of it. It feels like the truth and yet it also burns unnaturally. I remember that she glowed. She wore a white jumper that my father had bought her for Christmas. He'd hidden it in the loft and fetched it down in the afternoon, when it seemed as though all the gifts had been given that day. She exuded a childish joy and a faux outrage filled with love at the moment she realised that he'd bought it for her. A small but somehow important secret between them. A hint she'd thought had gone unnoticed. She wore faded jeans and a pair of slippers that I can't remember seeing before that day. They were grey with cartoon dog heads on them. A gift given long after I'd flown the nest. Her hair was still damp and unstyled in a manner that only her family were permitted to see.

She sat on her chair that faced the room – ever the hostess – and smiled at her beloved assembled cast. Behind the smile, which was genuine and warm and full of the love I'd felt from her my whole life, was a distant sadness. A far-away place where her father still lived. She held her coffee cup in both hands, her wedding ring clinking on the smooth ceramic surface as she felt the warmth radiate from within. 'World's Bestest Mum'. A Mother's Day gift from her young daughter nearly twenty years ago. As other cups had chipped and smashed and been replaced, this one had somehow remained as new. Her eyes shone as she spoke of things I can't recall. Gossip about the neighbours or affectionate barbs at my father's expense.

And the questions. Always the questions. A mother's need to know. A need to be a part of us always. To understand and share in our lives. If I could do so now, as I should have done that day, I would tell her that she never need doubt her place in our every breath. Our every thought belongs to her. Each action, each hesitation. Every success and every failure. Every smile is for her. She is etched into every fibre of our being. She is the reason and the light. Instead of saying this, I tutted and rolled my eyes. Playfully but with a note of caution that only she could read.

After coffee and biscuits, she sat next to Jen on the sofa and they cuddled up to each other. Just as they'd been doing ever since my memories began. Since my understanding of life had first formed into something tangible. A hug that lasted a girl's whole lifetime. Through sleepless nights and dirty nappies. Through tentative first steps and tantrums at the nursery gates. Through school uniforms and help with homework. Through 'Tidy your room!' and 'Eat your greens!' Through adolescence and hormones. Through boys and lipsticks and teenage disasters. Through coming home drunk and disrespecting your elders. Through standing ovations and the proud tears of graduation. Through abortion and darkness. Through the strength handed down to rise up and meet the new dawn.

Her love for us was the first thing I ever understood. It shielded me and encouraged me. It was with me through every dizzying high and crushing low. Without it, what would there be of me? What blank space devoid of colour and tomorrow's promise?

They fell asleep there on the sofa, in each other's arms. My father sat reclined in his chair until he too slipped quietly into the warm comfort of the abyss. All of them safe in the knowledge that they would awake to find their family surrounding them. Only I remained conscious then. A time when sleep would come to me so easily seemed now so far away as to itself be no more than a dream. I felt separate then. The three of them and me. But only for a whimpering second or two. Then I looked at my mother's sleeping face and saw that the whole world was at peace. That love would win the day in the end.

When the theme tune to *Antiques Roadshow* played out across the room, my mother awoke.

'Oh, goodness, is that the time? I'd better get those crumpets going or we'll never get to the cakes.'

She stretched and rose as Jen slumped down onto the cushion behind her. She smiled at me and ruffled my hair as she walked past. Then, as she left the room, she called to my father, 'Come on, mister, we've got the tea to make and I can see you're awake, thank you very much.'

My father mumbled under his breath and rose from his chair. He winked at me and smiled as he left the room. 'Sometimes I swear your mother's an alien that can read minds and see through walls.'

'I heard that!'

≡

I didn't know the significance of that day then. And so I cannot be sure of my recollection of it. It feels like the truth and yet it also burns unnaturally. I remember that when my father reappeared from the kitchen, carrying a plate piled high with buttery crumpets, he pretended to trip and almost spill them onto the carpet. He let out a playful cry and exclaimed that that had been a close one. He did this every Sunday without fail. Jen and I still laughed at it though, every single time. Because it was still funny. He placed the crumpets on the table and said the same thing he always said: 'Right, get your laughing gear round these, children of mine. It would've been nice if your mother had helped, but there you go.'

'Oh, now come on, we'll have none of that silliness today, thank you very much,' said my mother with the same playful roll of the eyes that she always gave at this moment. She carried a tray full of plates and cutlery, a jar of Marmite and another of jam.

'Oooh, Marmite, my favourite. Do you know, son, I've always thought you're a bit like Marmite?'

'Why's that, Dad?' I reply, already knowing the answer but dutifully setting up the punchline.

'Because I love you even though you smell bad.'

Later, in the evening, when the sun had gone down and Jen and I had given the first hints at needing to say our goodbyes, my father called me to one side.

'Come upstairs for a few minutes before you head off, son, I've got something to show you.'

As we walked up the stairs, I assumed that I was about to find out what my father's latest fad was. I expected to walk into the spare room to find it transformed into a dark room or artist's studio. Instead, as we crossed the landing, he turned to me with a look of concern etched across his face.

'I just wanted to check that you're okay.'

I was taken aback at first and then perhaps even a little annoyed. It felt for a second as though he was singling me out as the member of the family unable to cope with my grandfather's passing. Weaker somehow than my sister or my mother.

'I mean, I know we're all still missing your grandfather but that's not what I'm talking about. There's ... something else, right?'

'What do you mean, Dad?'

'I know my boy better than anyone and I know when something's not right. Is it Leon? Rolly? Or something else?'

I looked at him then. And I saw the worry written all over his features. I hugged him without answering. A hug that lasted a whole boy's lifetime. Through sleepless nights and dirty nappies. Through my first word, 'Dada', and the laughter of delight at being hoisted onto the giant's shoulders. Through the racing driver collecting me from school and the giant's hand wrapped around mine, guiding me through the dust that would sting my eyes for days. Through the 'Don't tell your mother' and 'Do what your mother says'. Through daddy's boy to the nightmare teenager that drifted away. Through the late-night phone calls for help and all the advice unheeded. Through watching the back of his head through the rear window of the vehicle in front, with the twisting turning road beyond. My guide, showing me the way once again. Picking me up when I fell and carrying me home when I was too weak to manage it under my own steam. Through the hero, the teacher, the father and the best friend.

'It's nothing, Dad. But thank you. Just a bad day, that's all.'

He wore a cotton shirt with the sleeves rolled up. I remember the feel and smell of it. I remember knowing that he didn't believe me. Understanding that, like my mother, he could read minds and see through walls where his children were concerned.

Jen and I left together as she was staying at my and Leon's house that night. I remember reversing the car down the driveway as my parents stood at their front door, under the glare of the porch lamp. I remember them smiling and waving, like they always did. I remember it was cold and the windscreen steamed up. I remember Jen waved back to them from the passenger seat as I looked behind me and manoeuvred the car onto the road. I remember the road was empty. Deserted and silent. A void. Then I turned towards them one last time before driving away. I remember their faces at that moment. I remember them smiling and waving, like they always did. I didn't know the significance of that day then. And so I cannot be sure of my recollection of it. It feels like the truth and yet it also burns unnaturally.

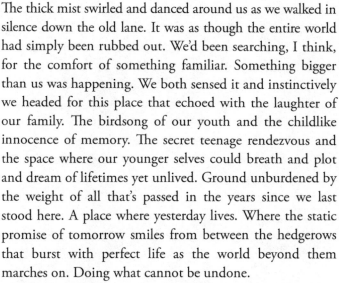

The thick mist swirled and danced around us as we walked in silence down the old lane. It was as though the entire world had simply been rubbed out. We'd been searching, I think, for the comfort of something familiar. Something bigger than us was happening. We both sensed it and instinctively we headed for this place that echoed with the laughter of our family. The birdsong of our youth and the childlike innocence of memory. The secret teenage rendezvous and the space where our younger selves could breath and plot and dream of lifetimes yet unlived. Ground unburdened by the weight of all that's passed in the years since we last stood here. A place where yesterday lives. Where the static promise of tomorrow smiles from between the hedgerows that burst with perfect life as the world beyond them marches on. Doing what cannot be undone.

The comfort and the answers we sought were not there that day. Or at least, the mist was keeping them hidden from us. It gave us no space, no room to breathe. Instead, it suffocated us with its cold blank canvas. We'd been carried there on a false promise and now could not see, in any sense, the way forward. No conversation about our grandfather. About how we missed him and how the world without him was a desperate, useless and ugly place. No discussion about the crushing disappointment of her attempts to trust someone again and find something more meaningful than brief encounters. No sharing of joy at the news of her landing the role of a lifetime and the fear of failure that threatened to bury alive the hope of a dream realised. No confiding in my oldest confidante about the pending collapse of the relationship that I had been so sure was forever. No talk of the best friend I'd lost and the hole it had left at my very core. Mill Lane had vanished and it left us in a silence as heavy as the whiteness that enveloped us.

We walked on, side by side. Not transported to the comfort of the past as we had hoped but rather removed from time altogether. There was only the two of us and the blank mist. No way forward, no way back. Everything and everyone besides the two of us seemed no longer to exist. Our memory knew the way. We still turned at the bends. The lane still gently rose and fell, meandering through the nothingness. But it was empty now. Bereft of reason. No life, no colour, no song.

After a time, the unease began to lift slightly. We were not alone in this, because we were together. She reached for my hand and we carried on with our fingers entwined. The sensation of touch the only evidence of reality left. Time itself began to melt away. How long had we been here now? Why was there no sound at all? Had the world really vanished, leaving only the two of us? Was this a dream? If so, was it mine or hers? Had we always been here, on this lane, hand in hand? This mist, what lay beyond it? The truth or a lie? As we walked, we became comfortable in our solitude. Perhaps this was all we needed. If we could not see it or hear it, then it could cause us no pain. We are hand in hand, we are as one in this. The past is lost, the future is a lie. This is where we are now. As long as we stay here, together, we are safe.

It was no longer the empty mist that held fear for us but rather its clearing. At the end of the lane ... what then? We sensed each other's fear and gripped hands more tightly. Suddenly the cold vacant mist was a warm blanket. It would keep us safe and warm and sheltered from the storm of that other distant place. But the creeping fear would not lie quiet in the folds of the mist. The security of its simplicity was temporary. We knew it. We felt it. We were the fear. A distant thread of understanding relayed the terrible truth. The lane was reaching its conclusion and we would have to leave this place. The promise of tomorrow was static no longer and bared its teeth as we held each other's hands so tightly that the nails drew blood.

I don't know what this was. Or even if it was. Did we know what lay ahead on some deep, wild, untamed level of our being? Our souls entwined so tightly that they drew blood. A glimpse of the depth of my own self-pity or a pre-emptive sign of how to escape it. Either, both, neither. She knows, understands. She is the truth beyond the mist, beyond the void. All that matters when the colour is lost, when the song has ended, is her. My sister.

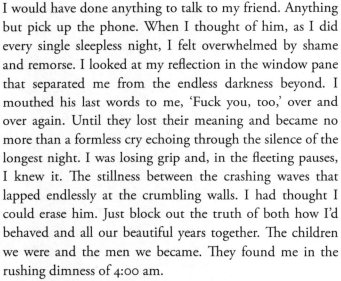

I would have done anything to talk to my friend. Anything but pick up the phone. When I thought of him, as I did every single sleepless night, I felt overwhelmed by shame and remorse. I looked at my reflection in the window pane that separated me from the endless darkness beyond. I mouthed his last words to me, 'Fuck you, too,' over and over again. Until they lost their meaning and became no more than a formless cry echoing through the silence of the longest night. I was losing grip and, in the fleeting pauses, I knew it. The stillness between the crashing waves that lapped endlessly at the crumbling walls. I had thought I could erase him. Just block out the truth of both how I'd behaved and all our beautiful years together. The children we were and the men we became. They found me in the rushing dimness of 4:00 am.

Beyond the selfish act of missing him. Beyond the need to both share with him this suffocating load and to feel the liberating warmth of his forgiveness. Beyond my own need and guilt, there was my love. All that he faced then was so vast and real. I yearned to know that he was okay. To be there when he was not. To stand by his side and meet the forces of time and circumstance together. As one. But not enough to pick up the phone.

Jen had spoken to Rolly at my grandfather's funeral, all that time ago. She didn't know why we weren't talking to each other. Nobody other than the three of us did. They'd not repeated what they'd told me that afternoon to anyone.

Jen told me that he seemed fine. That he was deeply sorry to hear about my grandfather's passing and honoured to have been given the opportunity to pay his respects at the funeral. Jen and Tabs had spoken separately too, about Rolly's state of health. I think Jen was on a factfinding mission for me and I'd guess Tabs probably knew it. He was doing fine. The medication was still working and things weren't progressing as quickly as they once had been. He was strong. Jen said that Tabs repeated that last point one too many times. I don't know if the subtext was intended to put my mind at rest or be a show of defiance. Perhaps both. I'd heard rumours from mutual friends that they might be leaving London, moving back home. Or even to Bristol. The sliver of opportunity coughed into the silence. A pathway leading to a workable future. A reason to keep fighting the oncoming storm. It sparked something in me. But not enough to pick up the phone.

In the face of what was to come, could my friend have prevented me slipping over the edge? I didn't know. I knew he'd have tried though. I knew he'd never have walked away from me when I needed him. I knew he was an infinitely better man than I. I knew he'd told me the truth that afternoon. Despite how hard it must have been for him to do so. Despite the fear that I'd react exactly as I did. Despite the fear that telling me might mean losing me. Because he will have known it. He understood the toxic rancidness of my weaknesses and he stood up to face them anyway. He met them with his honesty and love. As it was, he was not there when everything came crashing down. When the voice at the end of the phoneline screamed the unimaginable truth. The end of the world. The end of everything.

＝

I almost didn't notice when he finally left. He'd packed his bags and nearly managed to walk out without even saying a word.

'Where are you going?'

He didn't answer but instead just stood there in our semi-decorated hallway and stared at me. The contempt I'd seen looking back at me from those large hazel eyes, flecked with dancing orange, was gone now, replaced by something infinitely worse. Pity. Not the pity of a partner watching their beloved in pain. This was a pity devoid of any genuine concern. The pity that the privileged feel as they walk past a homeless person sitting huddled under a blanket on their daily commute. They may hand them some loose change, but they'll be sure not to touch skin or get drawn into conversation.

'Who is he?'

He smiled and shook his head at this, then turned to go.

'Please, don't do this.'

'Don't do this? We're a few years beyond "don't do this", aren't we?'

'Leon, I just need to … you can't go when I'm … I just need your help.'

'I know that. You've always needed that. Every single day since I first laid eyes on you. But that's not … I don't want to help you anymore. I want to be happy.'

He looked at me then and I thought I saw a flicker of something. One final invitation to say something that might stop this happening. A five-second window to find within myself the impossible words that might make everything alright. Or perhaps I imagined it. In any case, I had no words. I hated him at that moment. Even through that hatred a part of me still wanted to break down at his feet. To beg him to stay. To make a million promises I could never keep. But I didn't.

'I've taken Icarus. He's already at … he's already gone. It seemed, well, you know…' And with that he picked up his bags and left.

I didn't cry right away. I allowed my bitterness to take control, willing it on. As I turned to walk towards the kitchen, I caught a glimpse of myself in the mirror and stopped to look at it. There it was. The real source of my hatred. That pathetic runt of the litter. Would I want to live with that? But the more I stared, the less I saw. The features began to fade and the face staring back at me became a featureless barren landscape. The layers were stripping away and what if there was nothing underneath? No core. No essence.

In the kitchen, I switched on the kettle but before it finished boiling, I changed my mind. I opened a cupboard and pulled out a bottle of whisky. An expensive single malt that Leon's father had bought us as a Christmas present last year. I poured some into one of the tumblers made from Bristol Blue Glass that we'd picked out together at the fancy shop in Clifton, in another lifetime, and sat down at the table. That's when I saw the envelope. A brown A5 rectangle with my name scribbled on it in Leon's handwriting. I opened it with the sense of frustration that was ready to spill over into anger. But the letter within was far from what I had been expecting. Although it had been written earlier that day, the words were not those of the man I'd just watched walk out of my life, but those of a much younger man I'd once known many years ago. He'd been awakened from whatever forgotten part of Leon's consciousness he'd been cast out to, summoned to say goodbye to the boy he once loved.

Hello dearest,

Well, where to begin? Where did it all go so wrong? We were happy in the beginning, weren't we? Back when the very sight of you would send me into a wonderful incoherent stupor. When the very idea of you would make the whole world seem a sweeter place. Do you remember the old flat? I will remember those years always. Our nest. Hidden from the world. But, alas, the world found us in the end. I suppose I just want you to know that I have not forgotten what we once were to one another. I never will. Never could. I don't regret a single moment, my dearest.

Somewhere on our journey we lost each other. Our love flew away from us. But I don't say that with any bitterness or coldness in my heart. In the sober light I have only good thoughts for you, my dearest. I only hope with all my spirit that you find the happiness you deserve one day. The world is not as dark a place as you have come to believe. Remember the good times.

Always,
Leon

I did cry then. Not for the man who'd cheated on me and walked out on me but for the two boys in the flat above the greasy spoon café in London. They lived in a secret world with only two inhabitants. They smoked and laughed and watched the world go by.

I'd almost passed out on my chair when I heard the phone ring. I instinctively reached for my pocket but it was empty. I drunkenly followed the noise until I found it down the side of the sofa. When I answered it, I could hear Jen through the tinny speaker. She was screaming.

X

I sense her before I see her. I open my eyes and there she is, smiling at me with tears rolling down her cheeks.

'Jen?'

'Hello, bro.'

I cry. Again. It's all I'm good for.

'I'm so sorry, Jen.'

'Sssshh, I know.' She puts her arms around me and we hold each other for a lifetime. For two lifetimes shared. From birth to this moment, we hold each other. When the mist clears, she pulls away and looks at me.

'Where have you been?'

'I ... I don't know. I just couldn't...'

'I thought you were–'

'I know, I'm *so* sorry.'

'You just disappeared. Right when we ... for three weeks, not a word.'

I looked at her then, confusion washed over me. 'Three weeks? What do you mean, three weeks?'

'You've been missing three weeks, bro.'

Silence filled the space until ... I laughed. I laughed and could not stop.

'What the fuck is funny?'

But I really couldn't stop. I bent double and laughed until my ribs ached. A laugh that morphed into a broken, wretched sob. 'Three weeks? I thought I'd been gone months ... years ... decades ... forever. Three weeks!'

Three weeks outside of time. What lay beyond the mist

was the twisting darkness of the void. The empty cruelty of nothingness. Without them, I ceased to be. But then the weight of my guilt burst inside my belly like an ulcer. I left her there. My sister. I had left her in hell, alone, to face both our demons. And from the pit of that grief, she had to rise up and search for me. To drag herself up its rotting, screaming sides until her fingernails drew blood. When all she wanted was to hold me. For us to share this pain and find a way through together. To walk the lane in the mist, hand in hand. Our souls entwined. But I denied her this. I left her broken and alone to face the devil. As her heart burned for them, she searched for me. I forced her into the void. A trail of mouldy, rancid breadcrumbs that led her to this room. To this shell of a man. Useless. Gutless.

'The funeral?'

'It was fine, I guess. I mean, hardly anyone was there, right. Lesley and bloody Wendy. It was at the crematorium where Grandpa…' She trailed off and I saw the pain scrawled across her face. 'I mean, I've got no fucking idea what they would've wanted and you were … fuck knows where, so, you know? I did my best.'

'Jen … I…'

But what words could there possibly be? I was no more than a helpless incoherent child in front of this woman. This soldier still fighting when all is lost. Still screaming at the night in defiance. She'd organised the funeral alone… There was no one else. She'd held it off for days in the hope that I'd come home but, in the end, she'd had to go ahead. A small cluster of people. Faceless names she'd gathered using their address books. She'd fielded the questions, smiled her thanks and read their eulogy. Alone. And then she looked for me.

And what now? Here I was. Her brother.

PART THREE

The truth, as I know it to be, is lacking in detail. Those able to put flesh on the bones of all that unfolded that day are gone. Or wished that they were. My mother and father were driving on the M5 when a lorry jackknifed, travelling at sixty miles per hour. They themselves were travelling at approximately seventy miles per hour when the collision happened. Mum was killed on impact. Instantly ... or so they say. The passenger side of the car bore the brunt of the initial impact and, beyond the split second of panic she will have felt as the lorry slid towards her, she wouldn't have known anything about it ... or so they say. All that had got her there, all life and love, extinguished in a heartbeat. Dad died within twenty minutes. Before they could cut him from the wreckage. He was conscious. He will have seen her. Beside him.

It made the news. Fatalities on the M5, all carriageways closed. Expect delays. The lorry driver's name was Simon. In the weeks that followed the accident, Simon fell to pieces ... or so they say. Those who investigated the accident unanimously concluded that he was blameless in every respect. A mechanical failure. No driver error. Nevertheless, his guilt consumed him and he too made the news following a failed suicide attempt. I wonder if he sees them when he closes his eyes. I wonder if he knows all our names. My name. My sister's.

In the void, my mum and dad were the screaming ghosts that waited for me in my nightmares. The brief moments when sleep found me. I could quiet their screams if I kept my eyes open. Let the silence flood the empty space. Since the mist cleared, I cannot think of anything but that day. I'm consumed by the missing details of it.

It was a new car. They'd only had it a few months. The old Ford Orion had finally gone to the great scrapheap in the sky. A red Volkswagen Passat. I only know it was a Passat because it said so in the newspapers and on the television. Passat means trade wind in German. I looked it up on the internet, although I don't know why. Something to do with a Greek God. Jen believes that they were going shopping in Exeter. Mum loved to window shop and stop for coffee and cake. Dad loved to look at the architecture of the old buildings in the city centre. His favourite was the museum and art gallery. They both loved to wander around the cathedral. Arm in arm. But we'll never really know where they were going.

I wonder what they spoke about in the car. What they listened to on the radio. Dad had his Tom Jones CD in the glove compartment but mum would never have…

If I'd had to sit through the Green, Green Grass of bloody Home one more time…

One more time. I wonder what made them smile that day. If they laughed. Argued. I wonder if he had a chance to weep for her. To hold her hand as he faded away.

I feel all the things that the void protected me from now. All of them at once. They dance and kick and writhe and sob. The fury. A rage so naked that I want to smash my head against the wall until my brain explodes through my skull. I want to find Simon and tear at his face until everything he ever was is just an open bleeding wound. I want to grab every single person in the entire world by the neck and scream into their stupid useless faces. Stop what you're fucking doing, please, please, please! They are gone. Can't you see that they are gone?

The sadness. Not the selfish sadness of the void but the aching sadness of loss. Sadness for them. Sadness for my sister. Sadness for all of us. Our story, our love. I miss them so completely now. So crushingly that it kills me over and over again. Eventually it will allow me to be reborn. But not yet.

Relief also. For small things. Relief that my grandfather is not alive to feel this fury and this sadness. Even envy of him. He only knew a world where this hadn't happened. Relief that Leon had already gone. The distraction of our toxic entwinement makes me feel sick to think of. But these are, of course, nothing really. They are gone. They are gone.

The void
The numbness
The lacking
The blankness
The darkness
The empty space

We are all different things to different people. Different versions of the truth. Different layers. From a very young age, my grandfather would put me on a pedestal. Even as a child I remember being inherently conscious of this. Aware that the person he believed me to be – the one he saw when he looked in my eyes – was better than the truth of it. More somehow. Then, as time passed and the years rolled by, I slowly became the person that he saw. But only when he looked at me. A version of me unique to our relationship. No less true or real than any other version of myself. It's just that that part of me belonged only to my grandfather. Then, when he passed away, I realised that that version of me had died with him. Never again would I be his grandson. Never again would he look upon me and see that version of myself that could only be seen by him. And so, a layer of me was gone forever, buried with the only man who knew its truth. The nine-year-old boy who ran away from home and the smiling teddy bear of a man whose arms he ran to were both gone. I would forever be missing this part of me. A numbness followed and when it cleared, I was lesser.

When I threw away the layer of myself that was Rolly's best friend, I was lesser still. That part of me born a lifetime ago, in a small windowless room beyond a bustling classroom, was gone. Lost.

'My daddy is a racing driver.'
'No, he isn't!'

'Is!'

'Yeah, well, my daddy's the arm-wrestling world champion.'

'Wow!'

This layer was joyful and adventurous. Wide-eyed and wild with expectation. But it was also tempestuous and fragile. The loyalty that defined it was strong on the surface, but cracked and compromised on the inside. This layer was not the equal of that part of Rolly that he had given me. When the rotten feeble truth at the core of this layer finally revealed itself, I lost a relationship and a part of me that carried more of life's hope and possibility than any other. The numbness that followed was deeper and darker and whispered terrible things.

My love was never a pretty thing. In all our days, Leon never once saw the best of me. His layer was a broken and twisted thing from the beginning. But it was pure. A part of me born from the numbness but fuelled by a passion that seemed to offer up the whole world. A tender honesty that overflowed with the wild absurdity of whispered promises beneath a sweat-soaked sunrise. That layer was a fire. Burning brightly but for the briefest time only. A naked flame in the raging storm. When he left and another layer disappeared forever, only half of me remained. The rest was the numbness now. I was lesser then than this life demanded.

Yet the layers that remained were the strongest of all. They did know the best of me. And the worst of me and everything in-between. Knew me, accepted me and loved me. They could read minds and see through walls. These were the layers that made me. Nurtured and cultivated me. These were the layers that carried no weakness at their core but rather a strength and love so powerful that they could chip away at the numbness until it shattered into a million fragments. Even in the darkness of the empty space, I knew I would one day find their light and it would guide me through the thick, swirling mist. Carry me beyond the reach of the terrible whispered things.

When my mother and father died, my core was revealed. Laid bare. And it was the void. The layers were stripped away and there was nothing beneath. No essence. No inner strength. Only a faceless howling chasm. It flooded me, all I ever was, and I was drowned without a fight. Without a struggle. The world was the night, the night was the void, and the void was all there was. All I was. All I had ever been beneath the layers. I ran into the void and hid. I floated between and through two cities. Two chapters of what had once been. And they showed me the depths of our blankness and the blankness of our depths. The empty space and the shadows that swallow life. That stifle its screams and obscure its chance. They showed me the whistling truth of the night.

But not every layer had been stripped away. When I saw those eyes, infected and weeping, I knew their sorrow. I felt it. It was my sister's light that I used that night. Her love that would not be left behind by all that was lacking in me. Her love that screamed across the empty space. It found me and I drowned in it without a fight. Without a struggle. Through it, I saw those eyes so lost and beautiful and I answered their question. I followed them through the void and they led me to her.

'It's okay … it's okay. I've got you, bro, I've got you.'
And what now? Here I am. Her brother.

PART FOUR

We walk along the featureless corridor hand in hand. Jen squeezes and smiles at me reassuringly. We follow a girl who looks to me like she should be in school.

'Now, I need to warn you, he's obviously been through a lot. He's not a happy pup at the moment. You need to prepare yourself for that, okay? He hasn't let any of us near him since he's been here. He looks very sorry for himself and ... well, poor little boy.'

The cages we walk past are full but mostly silent. Dogs sleeping or dosed up on painkillers. A recovery ward. My palms are sweaty, my mouth is dry. Then, there you are. I run to your cage and fall to my knees. You're cowering in one corner with your back to us. I call your name and you leap up like a coiled spring. You turn and howl at me, your tail wags and your back end does its involuntary dance of delight.

The girl gasps and puts her hand to her mouth. 'Oh my God, that's the first time I've seen him–'

'Open the door, please!' I yell at her. I say it too loudly, too aggressively. But she's smiling, almost laughing with delight as she opens the cage door and we leap at each other. You're wearing a plastic cone on your head to stop you pulling at the stitches and bandages that cover your bruised and battered body. I remove it and we hold each other. A hug for a shared lifetime outside of time. A hug that carries us through the darkness and the empty space. And here we are now. Together in the light that we made for each other. I kiss you and kiss you, as tears of relief and love stream down my face. You lick me and whimper with delight at being found again. I will never let you down like I did the others. I will protect you forever. I promise, I promise, I promise.

'Jen, this is Marmite. Marmite, this is my sister.'

Jen kneels down beside me and with watery eyes begins to stroke you. 'Hello, Marmite, it's very nice to meet you.'

You barely register her presence at first as you shake with joy and cover me in saliva. But then, seeming to take a cue from me, you lean into her and the two of you hug. Then the three of us are embracing and the girl is standing above us in tears. She calls to a colleague to come and see your transformation from broken mutt to joyful puppy.

'Jason! Jason, come and have a look at Marmite. You won't believe it.'

We remain in this three-way embrace for what feels like an age. And then we leave that place. Together.

Jen understands all that we are to each other. It was the breakthrough at the bedside. As I tried to explain my life outside of time. As she fought to hold back her anger and her relief. When I spoke of you, I sparked into life. Found a way through the mist. From the shadows and into the light. She saw it. Felt it.

We head back to the house that was once Leon's and mine. It's our house now. And you fill it. All its memories are wiped clean. I follow you as you explore your new sur-roundings. Sniffing every inch of carpet and furniture. Your tail hasn't stopped wagging for a single second since we laid eyes on each other. You storm up the stairs and down them again, knocking against every surface, the plastic cone clattering along in time with your tail as they bang against the walls. When you run into the kitchen, Jen has laid out a bowl of fresh water and another of dog food. Turkey and chicken in jelly. I put my arm around her and we stand and watch you devour the food and splash water across the chequered lino floor. Jen looks at me and then back at you.

'Welcome home, you two.'

At some point during the time I was missing, Jen moved herself into my house. I'm still fuzzy on the exact order of things. After trying to call me for all those terrible, desperate hours on end, she eventually spoke to Leon. When he told her that he'd left, she made a snap decision not to tell him what had happened. Figuring that the house was the most likely place for me to finally show my face, no doubt drunken and remorseful, she headed to Bristol. She grabbed her bags and left her rented London flat behind. She waited for me in my empty house. Alone and grieving. She never unpacked but camped in the living room. Sleeping on the sofa, surrounded by her bags and suitcases. For those few weeks she was all that was left of us. All the years of love and joy and worry and fighting and smiles and tears. Our family was now one abandoned soul, curled up like a foetus, in a silent house that was no longer a home. And there she waited. It was from that room that she organised our parents' funeral and it was on that sofa she slept after it took place. Her longest day. She was all that was left of us that day.

In the weeks that followed our reunion, we set about trying to make the house a home again. The three of us. In the night we wept and held each other. Said all the things that my weakness and lacking had prevented us from saying to each other in the hours and days and weeks after our parents died. In the morning, the sun would rise and we'd take Marmite round the park. He'd run and sniff and wag his tail endlessly. In the daytime, we'd try to speak of other things. We painted a room. We went to Ikea. We did admin. Jen officially moved in. We began to see a future. The three of us. Unconventional and without regard for anything beyond our immediate circumstances.

In the night and sometimes in the day, the mist would fall again. But we'd be ready for it each time. We'd hold hands until the nails drew blood, our souls entwined. The three of us. The mist would clear and we'd carry on. The weeks rolled into months. In the night we still wept and held each other. Still said all the things we needed to say. In the morning, the sun would rise and we'd take Marmite round the park. In the daytime, things slowly began to ... the mist would still fall, but each time it did we passed through it a little quicker. Began to remember the way. The scars it left were as deep as they'd always been but our resistance to that pain was strengthening.

One evening we sat, the three of us, eating dinner in front of the television. *Miss Marple* came on and instead of the mist falling, the sun rose. I told Jen about Dad secretly recording it and watching it after Mum had gone to bed. We remembered how much she'd loved those books. How there'd always be copies scattered about the house. She'd read each one a thousand times or more. And it made us happy to remember them then. Their smiles and the sound of their voices. And the mist no longer fell. In the night, we still wept and held each other and said all the things we needed to say. In the morning, the sun would rise and we'd take Marmite round the park. In the daytime we spoke of normal things. We went back to work. Jen got a temp job in an office until she felt able to start auditioning again. We'd alternately work from home so that Marmite was never alone. We'd call each other on our lunchbreaks to speak of normal things. Take turns to cook. Oven-ready pizzas and microwave curries became homemade casseroles and Jamie Oliver's crab linguine.

Jen began to see a few old friends. The ones who'd never stopped messaging and phoning to find out how she was, even when she didn't answer them for days or weeks or months. We'd have people round for dinner and Marmite would slobber over them and run around excitedly. Anna fell in love with him and would bring him treats and squeaky toys. Normal things. In the night, we still wept and held each other and said all the things we needed to say. But even as we said them, we knew the sun would rise. Marmite made friends with some other dogs in the park and we'd chat to their owners as the crazed mutts pelted around and played. Normal things. We hung pictures. A photograph of Mum and Dad above the fireplace. One of Grandpa at the top of the stairs. A cartoon sketch of Marmite that one of Jen's friends did for us. We made a home of that house, the three of us. We found our way through the mist. We filled the empty space.

'So, you know you're going to have to talk to Rolly at some point, right?'

We were sitting on the sofa with Marmite curled up between us. Jen was reading a book as I flicked idly through a magazine.

'Where did that come from?'

She rested the book on her lap and turned to face me with one eyebrow raised. 'Oh, come on, bro. It's so overdue.'

I looked at her for a few seconds before letting out a long sigh.

'He calls me, you know?' my sister then revealed.

'What?'

'Yep. Every couple of weeks. Just to see how we are … how you are, really. Although he'd never say it.'

'I don't believe it … why haven't you told me?'

'I'm telling you now. You weren't ready until now.'

'Why am I ready now?'

'You're looking at a music magazine from the nineties that suddenly appeared on our coffee table. You've read it about a billion times in the last five days.'

'Nonsense.'

'You're wearing your Carter USM T-shirt and keep talking about buying a pair of DMs.'

'I only said mayb–'

'You've recorded two different documentaries about Parkinson's and have watched them both more than once.'

'Well, I…'

'You miss him.'

I fell silent. Jen reached across and took my hand.

'You miss him and he misses you. We're going around to see him this Saturday.'

'This Saturday?'

'I arranged it with Tabs.'

'Jesus, sis.'

'You're welcome.'

Rolly and Tabs had moved to Bristol a few months earlier. Unbeknown to me but apparently not to anyone else, they were less than a twenty-minute walk away from our house. They'd bought a red brick terrace with a grubby white PVC front door. As we walked along the road, I became increasingly nervous. I knew I had to make things right with my friend. I couldn't just let him forgive me and carry on as though nothing had ever happened. Not this time. Jen sensed how nervous I was and held my hand tightly. Marmite knew it too and slowed to walk by my side, glancing up at me every few seconds.

It was Tabs who opened the door. A huge, loving grin spanned the width of her flushed, glowing face. Beneath a large, stretched old T-shirt that I recognised as one of Rolly's was a bump.

'Oh my God! Tabs, you're…'

And she was. They were. Rolly appeared behind her only a second or two later and they ushered us in. Jen had already known, of course. We hugged. We cried. We congratulated and smiled until it hurt. I introduced Marmite before he pelted off around the house excitedly, investigating all the new smells. Rolly seemed good. His speech was slow and considered, as were his movements, but he seemed strong and radiant with the possibilities of the future. Of fatherhood.

We talked. Tentatively at first but then more freely. Rolly told me all that had happened since we last saw each other.

The house move, the pregnancy and the sorrow that he had felt when he heard about my parents. He had loved them both dearly, he told me, with watery eyes and a tenderness so sincere that it almost broke me. I tried to explain… Everything.

'Listen, both of you. I need to…'

'Mate, you don't need to do anything. It's all–'

'No. Rolly, please, mate. I do need to. I really do.'

The room fell silent.

'I need to apologise to you both. But especially to you, Rolly. I've been a terrible friend. Just as I've been a terrible brother. I let you down. Twice. I know that you've forgiven me, but I don't deserve that. I really, really don't. I own my behaviour, Rolly. I need you to know that. No excuses. Jen was in just as much pain as I was but she stood and faced it. I ran. I always ran. I knew you were telling me the truth about Leon. I never doubted it for a second. But I ran anyway.

'I love you. I love you, Rolly, mate. You're my brother and I want to be there for you now like you've always been there for me. But I'm weaker than you. I own that too. I used to think that I needed to look after you. But it's always been the other way around and I see that now. And Tabs, I'm so sorry. I don't know how you don't hate me. You should do. But I love you too. You're the best thing that ever happened to the best friend anyone ever had. I love you both, and I'm so, so happy for you. You'll be the best parents any kid could ever have.

'But, anyway, that's not … I just need you to know that … that I know what I've done. I know how much I hurt you both. I carry it and I'll never forget it. Everything I love is in this room and I will never run again. I promise you all that. Okay?'

The three of them looked at each other as Marmite darted into the room and leapt up onto the sofa.

'Marmite, get down!' cried Jen.

'Oh, no, don't worry, it's fine,' Tabs replied.

Then Rolly leaned forward. 'Okay, mate. Thank you for saying that. And I love you, we love you too.'

'And we missed you,' added Tabs.

The tension lifted then and we laughed with a warm familiarity that filled the empty space a thousand times.

And that was that. Then came the future. Rolly and Tabs asked me to be the godfather of their child and I was overcome with joy at being asked. And then there was a new life. A new layer. Baby Abigail. With her father's smile and her mother's eyes.

I've been wrong all along, of course. Well, mostly. We are all different things to different people. And that each meaningful relationship we have should represent a layer of our own personality seems as reasonable and true a suggestion as any other I've come across. But we are more than the sum of these relationships. Our layers are many. And those layers of ourselves formed by our associations don't simply die when our loved ones do. I will forever be my grandfather's grandson. Nothing so trivial as time or mortality can change that. My mother and father are not merely reflections of the bonds that they forged with those around them. It is, in some way, insulting to their memory to suggest that they are that and that alone. There are millions of layers beyond those reflected in the eyes of our loved ones.

I see now that the void was a layer. Is a layer. No more, no less. Not a layer born from my connection to anyone else but something different. Perhaps nurtured by everything and everyone or perhaps not nurtured at all. Perhaps a layer that simply appeared when I did. Always in there somewhere. Lying dormant until circumstances give it the confidence to assert itself. To become the dominant layer. But I cannot hate the void because I am the void. It's as much a part of me as all the things that my loved ones see when they look at me. It's what I saw when I looked at myself.

The numbness was not trying to show me the horror that hides in the shadows. It meant only to cast a shadow over the terrible things I could not bear to face. To protect me from my inability to deal with the aching loss. My lacking. I'm lucky to have got as far into adulthood as I did before I lost anyone close to me. But the trade-off was that, when I did lose someone, I wasn't ready for it. The void wasn't ready. It didn't know how to protect me. It was a crude, unformed thing. An empty space. It panicked and spewed its darkness over everything.

It's still in there, resting. It will assert itself again someday. All our lives are filled with loss. It floods the empty space. But the void will learn and grow as I do. When it's next called upon it will be a different thing. There are and always will be dark corners in the void. It is the layer of me closest to the beast. To death. But it's still only a reflection. I have learnt from the void and it too will learn from the layers around it. The layers that grow and dance and laugh and cry. That howl at the night.

And so, life goes on. As it must. Each morning the sun will rise. I'm blessed – more blessed than most. I have the love of my family and friends. Past, present and future. They're all in there. The future is not a lie and its promises are not static. It learns and grows and writhes with excitement. The past is not dead, I promise, I promise, I promise. I am my best friend's best friend. I let him down and lift him up. I am all my lovers' desires. All their insecurities. We nurture and destroy each other to be born again and again and again. I am my sister's brother. I hold her hand so tightly that the nails draw blood. We lose each other but we find each other and the mist clears to reveal the way. I am my dog's master and he is mine. Our light protects each other from all the darkness of the world. I am my grandfather's grandson. I sit on that pedestal still. Each day I strive to be the man that he believed me to be. And every week I buy a